The Third Pig Detective Agency

The Third Pig Detective Agency

Bob Burke

FRIDAY
FICTION

The Friday Project
An imprint of HarperCollinsPublishers
77–85 Fulham Palace Road, Hammersmith, London W6 8JB

www.thefridayproject.co.uk
www.harpercollins.co.uk

First published by The Friday Project in 2009

1

Bob Burke asserts the moral right to be identified as the author of this work

A catalogue record for this book is available from the British Library

ISBN 978-1-906321-75-8

This novel is entirely a work of fiction. The names, characters and incidents
portrayed in it are the work of the author's imagination. Any resemblance to actual
persons, living or dead, events or localities is entirely coincidental.

Internal design and typesetting by Wordsense Ltd, Edinburgh

Printed and bound in Great Britain by Clays Ltd, St Ives plc

Mixed Sources

Product group from well-managed
forests and other controlled sources
www.fsc.org Cert no. SW-COC-1806
© 1996 Forest Stewardship Council

FSC

FSC is a non-profit international organisation established to promote
the responsible management of the world's forests. Products carrying the
FSC label are independently certified to assure consumers that they come
from forests that are managed to meet the social, economic and
ecological needs of present or future generations.

Find out more about HarperCollins and the environment at
www.harpercollins.co.uk/green

To Gem, for believing

Contents

1

A New Client

It was another slow day in the office. Actually, it had been a slow week in the office. No, if the truth be known, it had been a lousy month for the Third Pig Detective Agency. That's me by the way: Harry Pigg, the Third Pig.

Where did the name come from? Well, I was the pig that built the house out of bricks while my idiot brothers took the easy route and went for cowboy builders and cheap materials. Let me tell you, wood and straw ain't much use when Mr Wolf comes calling. Those guys were pork-chops as soon as he drew in his first breath and filled those giant lungs of his. Blow your house down, indeed.

And while we're on the subject, don't believe what you read in those heavily edited stories you find in children's books of fairy tales saying how the wolf fell down the chimney into the pot, scalded his tail, ran out of the house and was never seen again. When that wolf came down my chimney and into that boiling saucepan, I screwed the lid on and made sure it stayed on by weighing it down with a few spare bricks (never throw anything away, you never know when it could come in useful). He didn't do too much huffing and puffing then.

'Little pig, little pig, let me come out,' he'd begged in a scared whimper.

'Not by the hair on my...' I began, but then gave up. I just couldn't come up with something clever to rhyme with 'I won't let you out' so I just left it. Hey, I can't come up with a witty reply every time.

By the time the pot went quiet and I opened it again all that was left was some scummy hair floating on the surface and bones – lots of bones. The little dog sure laughed a lot that day. He hadn't seen that many broken bones since the cow's first attempt to jump over the moon, and they'd kept him in three square meals a day for over a week.

After that I was kind of a cult hero. Apart from that Red Riding Hood dame, no one else had ever come out on top in a skirmish with the Wolf family so I became a local celebrity. After the usual civic receptions and TV appearances, I decided to capitalise on my new-found fame and become a detective. Well, why not? Someone needs to do it and there's always an opening for a good one.

At first business was booming. I was the one who not only found those two missing kids, Hansel and Gretel, but I also fingered them for the murder of that sweet old woman in the gingerbread house. Their story was too pat: wicked old lady plans to eat the kids, only way out was to kill her; you know the drill. In my book their story stank. Two kids, a house made of gingerbread and an old dear whose only crime was to get in the way. It was always going to end in tears – primarily hers.

As I said, I was on the pig's back (excuse the pun) for a while but then things kind of dried up. No one seemed to want the services of a good detective agency and, with the exception of the kids in Hamelin (which wasn't even one of my cases), there didn't even seem to be too many missing persons any more. The bills were mounting up. Gloria, my bovine receptionist, hadn't been paid in a month. Even her legendary patience was wearing thin. And no, before all you politically correct fairy tale readers get on my case, I'm not casting any aspersions on her looks; she really is a cow and the meanest typist in Grimmtown (even with the hoofs). Unless I got a big case – and soon – I was going be neck-deep in apple sauce and Gloria would be back to cheerleading for the Lunar Leapers Bovine Acrobatics Team. Things were most definitely not looking good.

But I digress (a little). On this particular slow day I was sitting in my office (cheap furniture, lousy décor, creaky wooden floor – you know the type) with my rear trotters on my desk, trying to work out 5 down. 'Sounds like fierce brothers in the fairy tale world. Five letters ending in 'm'. Hmmm.' I mulled this over while nibbling the end of my pen. Crosswords really weren't my strong suit.

As my creative juices attempted to flow I became aware of voices in the outer office. Voices meant more than one person, so Gloria either had a debt-collector or a potential customer on her hands – and there was no one in town more adept at evading debt-collectors than me. Once I heard her say, 'Mr Pigg is quite busy at present, but I'll see if he can squeeze you in', it meant an obviously discerning client wished to utilise my services. I swung my trotters off the desk, smoothed down my jacket as best I could and tried to look busy while squashing the newspaper into the wastebasket with my left trotter.

The intercom buzzed.

'Mr Pigg,' crackled Gloria's deep, husky voice. 'There is a gentleman here to see you. Should I get him to make an appointment?'

As my diary was conspicuously blank for the foreseeable future I figured that my need for hard cash far outweighed any need to impress a potential punter. I pressed the intercom button.

'I can see the gentleman now, Gloria,' I said. 'Please send him in.' I stood up to meet my potential cash cow.

Through the opaque glass in the connecting door, I could see a large shape making its way through reception and towards my office. The door slowly opened and an oriental gentleman the size and shape of a zeppelin entered. He was wearing a silk suit, the amount of cloth of which would have made easily the most expensive marquee tent in history, and he was weighed down with enough gold to pay off all of my debts for the next twenty years. His shiny black hair was pulled back from his forehead and tied in a long plait that stretched all the way down his back to a voluminous rear end. The guy exuded wealth – and I hadn't failed to notice it. If this were a cartoon, dollar signs would be going 'ka-ching' in my eyes.

It was time to be ultra-smooth, ultra-polite and ultra-I'm-the-best-detective-you're-ever-likely-to-meet-and-you-will-be-eternally-grateful-for-employing-me.

I extended my trotter, 'Mr?'

'Aladdin,' he replied, grasping my trotter in a grip like a clam's. 'Just call me Mr Aladdin.'

Although I didn't recognise him, of course I had heard of Aladdin. Everyone in Grimmtown had. He was probably the most famous and most reclusive of our many eccentric citizens – and quite possibly the richest. Rumour had it he owned half of the town but very few people had seen him in recent years, as he preferred to live behind closed doors in a huge mansion in the hills.

His story was the stuff dreams (at least other people's dreams) were made of. He had started off working in a local laundry. After a few years he bought out the owner although no one knew, despite much speculation and rumour, where the money had come from. Over the years his business had expanded (as had he) and he had begun to diversify. Apart from the chain of laundries he had built up, he owned bars, restaurants, department stores, gas stations and most local politicians. The key word in the above description is, of course, 'richest'. If Mr 'Just call me' Aladdin wanted to employ my services, it would be most churlish of me to turn him down – especially if he was prepared to throw large wads of cash in my direction.

Ka-ching! Ka-ching!

I took a deep breath and prepared to tell my new best friend how wonderful I was and how he had showed exceptional judgement in availing himself of my services.

'Mr Aladdin, how may I be of service?'

That's me: cool and straight to the point. Inside, my mind was screaming, 'Show me the money', and I was trying not to dance on the table with joy.

Mr Aladdin looked carefully at me, raised his left hand and snapped his fingers.

'Gruff,' he said. 'My bag, please.'

Someone, hidden up to now by his employer's large mass, walked out from behind him carrying a large leather, and undoubtedly very expensive, briefcase. My heart sank. Things had just started taking a turn for the worse. It always happens to me. Just when I think things can't get any better, they inevitably don't and take another downward slide into even more unpleasantness. Aladdin's employee was a sturdy white goat. Not just any goat however, this was a Gruff. And, unless I was very much mistaken, he was the eldest Gruff.

The Gruffs were three brothers who had come to town a few years ago. After sorting out a little (well big, actually) troll problem we were having at a local bridge (a trollbridge, if you will), they had decided to stay and give the town the benefit of their 'unique' skill set – which usually involved threats, intimidation and the carrying of blunt instruments. Starting out as bouncers at 'Cinders', one of Grimmtown's least reputable clubs, they had subsequently branched out into more profitable (and much less legal) operations. Whether it was smuggling live gingerbread men across the border or evicting the old lady in the shoe for not paying the rent, the three billy goats Gruff were usually involved in some capacity.

Eventually the eldest brother had distanced himself from the day-to-day operations of the family business. I'd heard he'd gone into consultancy of a sort usually described as 'security', but not much had been seen of him recently. Now I knew why. If he was employed by this particular client, I suspected he worked for him to the exclusion of any others. Mr Aladdin was that kind of employer; apart from total commitment, it was rumoured he also demanded total secrecy from his staff. If Gruff was involved, it stood to reason that there were some less than legal factors of which I was yet to be made aware.

Wonderful!

Gruff handed the briefcase to his boss and looked me up and down.

'I don't like you,' he sneered.

I shrugged my shoulders. 'You don't like most people.'

'But I especially don't like pigs.'

7

'Well then, perhaps you'd be more comfortable somewhere else – an empty shoe, a prison cell, maybe propping up a bridge somewhere?'

Snarling, he made to move towards me but his employer restrained him with a large and heavily bejewelled hand. With that amount of rings on his fingers it was a wonder he actually had the strength to lift it.

'Gentlemen, please. Enough of this petty squabbling! Gruff, keep an eye on the door, will you? There's a good goat.'

Reluctantly the goat backed towards the door, never taking his eyes off me. I met his gaze all the way. No goat was going to outstare me.

Happy that his employee was a safe (or at least a less-threatening) distance away, Aladdin turned towards me.

'Might we continue?' he said.

'Of course,' I replied, returning to my chair while, at the same time, ensuring that a large and heavy desk was strategically placed between a highly unstable goat and me. Picking up a letter opener in as non-intimidating a fashion as possible, I began to clean my front trotters and looked expectantly at Aladdin.

'Mr Pigg,' he began. 'You have a reputation as a man – I apologise, of course I mean pig – who not only gets results but knows when to be discreet.'

I nodded politely at the compliment.

'In my experience, an indiscreet detective doesn't stay in

business too long,' I pointed out.

'Nevertheless,' he continued, 'in this particular instance, discretion is of paramount importance. I must insist that you do not discuss what I am about to reveal with anyone other than my associate Mr Gruff, and me.'

I nodded, wondering what was going to come next.

Opening the briefcase, Aladdin took out a large sheet of paper. 'I have recently mislaid an item of immense personal value and I wish you to locate it for me.'

He handed the sheet of paper to me. I looked at it with interest. It was a photograph of a very old and very battered lamp.

'It's a lamp,' I said, stating the blindingly obvious.

'Not just any lamp,' said Aladdin. 'This is a family heirloom and one which I am most anxious to have located as soon as possible.'

'Where was it mislaid?' I asked.

'It was last seen in a display cabinet in my study. Last night it was most definitely there; this morning it was gone.'

'Lost? Stolen? Melted down and sold for scrap? Can you be a little more specific?' I looked at the picture again. The lamp didn't look up to much. It was about the size of a gravy boat, coloured an off-shade of gold and had more dents than the Tin Man. I clearly needed more information.

'I... ah... suspect it may have been stolen but I am unable to prove this at present.'

'Have you spoken to the police?'

Again, rumour had it that local law enforcement was more akin to Aladdin's private security force than public servants. If anyone could locate an artifact of this nature quickly and with a minimum of fuss, it was them. In all likelihood, their jobs would depend on it.

Aladdin looked at me carefully. 'The police have been more than helpful but, at this time, they have neither a suspect nor a specific line of inquiry. It is my firm belief that someone of your talents might be of more use in this particular instance.'

'Because?' I enquired.

'Because, as I have already mentioned, you can be discreet. I think that perhaps you can exploit particular avenues of inquiry that may be outside the scope of the law and you have your snout in all the right information troughs – forgive the analogy, I mean no offence.'

'None taken,' I replied. Offended or not, I wasn't going to abandon this client just yet, certainly not on the basis of a less than politically correct analogy. 'However, I don't normally take on cases that are still under investigation by the police.'

'Trust me,' came the very smooth reply. 'The police have exhausted all avenues and will not bother you during the course of your investigation.'

In other words they'd come up with nothing – or at least nobody they could pin the theft on. Either that or this lamp was something that Aladdin would prefer not having the police involved with. This case stank higher than an abattoir in a heatwave – and I should know, my office looks out on one and it wasn't a nice place to be in the summer.

My only question now was should I take this particular case on? If the lamp had been stolen, chances were that someone with more than a passing grudge towards Aladdin had taken it. By extension, they were probably not nice people. Not nice people didn't normally worry me – in my line of work I come across quite a few – but I suspected this particular category of not nice people probably wouldn't have too many qualms about serving me up for breakfast along with some scrambled eggs. I decided cowardice was the better part of valour in this instance.

'Mr Aladdin, I'm flattered that you saw fit to choose the Third Pig Detective Agency but I don't think I'm in a position to take you on at the moment. My caseload is somewhat heavy.'

He looked at me extremely carefully. 'I think, perhaps, you might reconsider,' he said, very quietly but very ominously.

'No, really. It's just not possible right now. I am sorry.'

Aladdin turned to his henchgoat. 'Mr Gruff?'

Gruff opened the briefcase again and took out a large folder which he handed to his employer. He was smiling at me as he did so.

Aladdin opened the folder and began to flick through the pages. 'Mr Pigg, what I have here, among other things, are your last six bank statements, a number of bills from certain of your suppliers – most of which are, apparently, very overdue – and a number of demands for rent, which seems considerably in arrears. Your former landlord seems particularly unhappy with you.'

I was about to launch into a robust defence of my financial situation, which would include claims of invasion of privacy, how unjust certain of my suppliers were in their demands and how things weren't actually as bad as they looked, when the last part of his statement suddenly sunk in.

'Former landlord?' I said.

'Oh yes, didn't I mention? As of...' he glanced at his watch, 'forty-five or so minutes ago, I now own this building. You appear to owe me quite an amount of rent.' He handed the folder back to Gruff. 'Shall I have Mr Gruff here organise for collection? I do believe he is a most effective debt-collector. I certainly haven't had any complaints about his methods.'

That sealed it for me. I could have lived with owing half of Grimmtown money and having Aladdin as my new landlord, but I wasn't going to give the goat the satisfaction of coming around with a large baseball bat to collect any outstanding rent.

With as much dignity as I could muster, I caved in.

'Mr Aladdin, you are a most persuasive client. I assume you would like me to start immediately?'

Aladdin smiled at me. It was the kind of smile that suggested one of his grandparents was a shark.

'Delighted to hear it. If you need anything, Mr Gruff will be more than happy to accommodate you.'

I decided to make Gruff suffer a bit. 'I'd like to see where you kept the lamp. Can your goat make himself available to show me around?'

The expression on Gruff's face at this comment suggested that he'd sooner play catch with dynamite. Hey, it was a small victory but I had to take 'em where I got 'em.

Aladdin was heading for the door. Barely looking over his shoulder he asked – no, told – me to call at the house at twelve the next day and Gruff would show me around.

As the door closed behind him I sank back down into my chair and exhaled loudly. My client was now my landlord. He was missing something that he wanted to get back badly. He wanted little or no involvement with the law and, for reasons known only to himself, he had chosen me rather than any of the other detectives operating in town to do the recovery. Sometimes I just got all the breaks.

'Oh Harry, Harry, Harry,' I breathed. 'What kind of mess have you gotten yourself into now?'

2
Come Blow Your Horn

I f television is to be believed, we detectives have contacts everywhere. All it takes is a quick phone call to Izzy or Sammy or Buddy and, hey presto, there it is - information at your fingertips. Barmen, bouncers, paperboys, waitresses; you name them, your average detective has them in his little black book. They have their ears to the ground and are always willing to give exactly the information you're looking for exactly when you need it, in return for a small fee.

Wrong!

Forget what you see on TV. Most detectives I know, myself included, can muster up one informant if we're really lucky; usually unreliable, rarely cheap and never around when you want them. My particular source of 'useful' information was a lazy former shepherd. He had got himself into a spot of bother when - after falling asleep on the job one day - his flock had disappeared. Blacklisted and unable to hold down any other kind of agricultural employment, he eked out a living playing the trumpet in some of the town's cheaper bars. He usually then spent the money drinking in the same bars. When people talked of someone with his ear to the ground they meant literally in his case. He did get around, however, and if something was going on in town, there was always the remote possibility he might have heard about it. More than likely, however, he hadn't.

When not performing, he was usually found in Stiltskin's Diner nursing a cup of espresso and a hangover. Stiltskin's was that kind of diner – great coffee, but the sort of food that was described in books about poor children in orphanages as 'gruel'. Regardless of what you asked for it was inevitably served up as a grey lumpy mass – quite like the diner's owner, in fact. Rumpelstiltskin was surly, rarely washed and had all the customer service skills of a constipated dragon. In his defence, however, he did serve the best coffee in Grimmtown.

Well, he had to have one redeeming feature.

I entered the diner and headed for the counter.

'Blue here?' I asked, trying to ignore the smell.

Rumpelstiltskin was cleaning a glass but from the state of the cloth he was using I suspected all he was doing was adding more dirt to an already filthy inside. He grunted in reply and nodded towards a booth at the back of the diner.

'You are as gracious as you are informative,' I said. 'Any chance of a coffee, preferably in a clean mug?' I looked pointedly at what he had in his hands.

Another grunt, which I assumed was an affirmative, but it was hard to tell.

I made my way to the back of the diner. It was a little early for the evening rush but some tables were already occupied. A few construction trolls were sharing a newspaper, or at least looking at the pictures. They also seemed to be the only ones eating what might have been loosely described as a hot meal. That was the thing about trolls: they were a chef's delight. They ate anything thrown up in front of them (and my choice of phrase is deliberate), never complained and always came back for seconds. They single-handedly kept Stiltskin's in business – and they had very big hands.

My contact was sitting in a darkened booth and barely acknowledged me as I sat down. He was still wearing that ridiculous bright blue smock and leggings that all our shepherds wore. The only sop to his status as a musician was a pair of sunglasses.

'Blue,' I greeted him. 'How're tricks?'

He grunted once and continued to nurse his coffee. It was obviously a day for grunts. Conversation wasn't his strong point either. It seemed to be a feature of the people who frequented Stiltskin's.

'I'm looking for information,' I said.

'Ain't you always,' came the reply. He still hadn't bothered to look up.

I pressed on regardless. 'Rumour has it that one of our more upstanding citizens has lost something valuable. He seems to think I might be able to help him locate it. I figured if anyone had heard anything on the grapevine, it'd be you.'

'Anyone I know?'

'That stalwart of Grimmtown high society, our very own Mr Aladdin,' I replied.

At the mention of Aladdin's name he suddenly became less disinterested. He sat upright so fast it was like someone had pumped 5,000 volts through him. Now I had his complete and undivided attention.

'Well, well. So he's come to you, eh? Must be scraping the bottom of a very deep and very wide barrel.'

I ignored the insult. 'He obviously appreciates the skills that I provide... and I appreciate the skills that you provide,' I said, slipping a twenty-dollar note across the table to him. There was a blur of movement and the note disappeared off the table and into his pocket. I'd have sworn his hands never moved.

He leaned forward so much our heads were almost touching. 'Word on the street is he's missin' his lamp,' he whispered. 'Not good from his point of view.'

'Yeah? Why's that? What's so special about it?'

Boy Blue leaned even closer, pushed his shades up onto his forehead and, for the first time since I had arrived, looked directly at me. His eyes were an intense blue – just like his ridiculous outfit.

'Rumour has it that it's a magic lamp and he somehow used it when he was younger to make himself very rich.

'There he was, didn't have two coins to rub together, working for peanuts in a laundry. Suddenly he was the talk of the town, appearing at all the best parties, escorting dames like Rapunzel; quite the overnight sensation.'

I groaned inwardly. Magic! I hated magic. As a working detective it's bad enough running the risk of being beaten up or thrown into a river with concrete boots on, without having to live with the possibility of being changed into a dung beetle or having a plague of boils inflicted on you. If you think humans were disgusting covered with boils, imagine how I might look. No! Magic was to be avoided where possible and if it had to feature in a case, I wanted the Glenda the Good type – the type that had lots of slushy music and sparkly red slippers. With my luck, however, this was probably going to be the other type. I was already having premonitions of waking up with the head of a hippo and the body of a duck, going through the rest of my life only being able to grunt and quack.

'Any idea if this magic lamp actually worked?' I asked.

'Nah. I don't even know if it's true. You know how these things are – he probably arrived in town in a stretch limo and with a pocketful of dough. Twenty years later, the rumour becomes the truth because it's just so much more romantic.' He laughed quietly. 'One thing's for sure though, he's certainly not a man to be messed with. He has some interesting hired help.'

'I know. I think I got off on the wrong trotter with one of them this morning.'

'Big guy, scruffy white beard, perpetually angry and smells of cheese?'

'Yeah, that's the fellow; the inimitable Mr Gruff. We've had run-ins before.'

Boy Blue swallowed the dregs of his coffee and pushed the cup away. He belched loudly and with great satisfaction. 'Amazin' thing about this place: lousy food, great coffee. Didn't think it was possible.'

'Well think about it,' I replied. 'Stiltskin's got to have something going for him – apart, of course, from his scintillating personality. But let's get back to Aladdin.' I tried to gather my thoughts. 'Thing is, why would anyone want to steal this lamp, if the story about it is, in fact, just that – a story? Can't see this particular gentleman being overly upset at the thought of having a family heirloom stolen – certainly not upset enough to hire me. It certainly didn't look valuable from the photo he showed. Then again, what do I know? I'm no antiques expert.'

Boy Blue's eyes didn't so much as flicker. 'What if the story's true? Think about it, what could someone do with a magic lamp?'

I thought about it. More to the point, I thought about what I could do with a magic lamp – and I didn't have too fertile an imagination: big house, big car, gold-plated – maybe even pure gold – feeding trough. One rub and all my troubles would be over and, before you ask, it's a convention in this town: you always rub any brassware you might find on the street, just like you always wave any ornate stick when you pick it up and always click your heels together when wearing any kind of sparkly red jewelled shoes. I may not like magic but that's not to say there isn't a lot of it about and people certainly know how to check for it.

It also hadn't escaped my notice that if the wrong people got their hands on this particular source of untold wealth and power then it could create quite a lot of problems – assuming it was the genuine article. There were too many stories of people in Grimmtown who bought pulse vegetables from total strangers with the promise of great things happening to them. With the exception of a guy called Jack (another client whose story I must tell you someday), these great things didn't ever amount to much more than a hill of beans, unless you happened really to like eating vegetables.

My chat with Boy Blue, however, gave me the distinct impression that we were dealing with the bona fide article and a client who wanted it back urgently – presumably before someone else could do what he did all those years ago. Even worse, maybe they had stolen it to use against him. Even worse again, he had hired me to get it back. Ah yes, things were definitely on the expected downward spiral. This was turning out to be a typical Harry Pigg case: much more trouble than it was worth, the potential for great harm being inflicted upon me, and probably impossible to get out of unless I actually found the artifact. I seem to attract these cases like a cowpat attracts flies.

I turned my attention back to Blue, who had now started on my coffee. 'Don't suppose you've any idea who might have taken this lamp?'

'Take the phone-book; stick a pin anywhere in it. Chances are you've found a likely suspect.' He leaned back and looked at the ceiling. 'Any idea how it was stolen?'

'I'm going out to Casa Aladdin tomorrow to have a look. It strikes me that it must have been a professional job. I imagine a man like him would have state-of-the-art security. Someone that rich with something he treasured that much is hardly likely to keep it under his bed beside the chamber pot.'

'That narrows it down a little. Depending on how good his security system is you're lookin' for someone with enough dough to hire the right help, or the technical smarts to do the job themselves.'

I thought about it. 'Maybe, but if they had those kind of resources, they probably wouldn't need the lamp, would they?'

Blue sniggered. 'Think about it. Ever seen a Bond movie? The kind of guys who would want to steal this are probably thinking about taking over the world, not how they might put the owner of a laundry out of business. We're not talking washing powder and scruffy underwear here, we're talking big weapons, thousands of thugs with large guns, huge secret headquarters hidden under water. Think big and you have your likely villains.'

This really wasn't what I wanted to hear. I was hoping more for a pawnshop and an easy recovery not megalomania and superweapons. A small-time detective probably wouldn't have much of a chance against that kind of opposition – particularly not this small-time detective.

It was time to go and detect. I slid out of the booth and put my overcoat back on. 'Enjoy my coffee,' I said to Boy Blue. 'It's on me.'

He didn't acknowledge either my generosity or my departure. Typical informant!

I waved goodbye to Rumpelstiltskin on my way out and left the restaurant. Night was falling and, as I headed back to the office, I tried not to laugh out loud as Grimmtown's bright young things made their appearance. I'm no connoisseur of fashion, but to my non-discerning eye this autumn's look was clearly vampire. Lots of black: shoes, clothes, capes, lipstick, hair and eyes. In fact, if there hadn't been any street lights, it would have been difficult just to see them. But, unfortunately, you could still hear them and, in keeping with the theme, there were lots of 'velcomes', 'do you vant a drink' and other stupid vampire sayings from cheap Hollywood B-movies. Nothing like an idiotic trend to sent the fashionistas flinging themselves like lemmings over the cliffs of good taste. Six months from now it would probably be the Snow White look and Dracula would be 'so last year, darlink'.

Outside the Blarney Tone Irish bar, a small man in a bright green outfit was trying to entice customers inside to sample the evening's entertainment. At the Pied Piper Lounge a group of idiots dressed as rats tried to provide an exciting alternative to the more discerning client. It was just as well it was getting dark. No self-respecting punter would enter either premises if they had seen it in daylight.

A number of fast-food sellers were hawking their less than appetising wares on street corners. Hungry though I was, I restrained myself – rat-on-a-stick with caramel sauce didn't engage my senses as perhaps it should. It looked like another busy night in the town's social calendar and one I was, in all honesty, looking forward to missing – not being the social type at all.

I walked the mean streets of Grimmtown back to my office – the further I walked, the meaner they got. I turned into an alleyway that I frequently used as a shortcut. As Grimmtown Corporation hadn't seen fit to light up the alley, I made my way carefully along in the dark, trying not to kick over any trashcans (or any sleeping down-and-out ogres – they were never too happy when suddenly awoken).

As I stumbled along I became aware of a shuffling noise behind me. As a world-famous detective, I had developed a sense of knowing when I was being followed and now this spidey-sense was screaming 'Danger, danger, Will Robinson!' I spun around, trotters raised, ready to fight and, in the same fluid movement, flew backwards into the rubbish behind me when a large fist punched me powerfully in the stomach.

Gasping for breath, I shook old potato peelings and rotting fruit off my suit and slowly came to my feet, trying to see who had hit me. In the darkness I could barely make out my fists in front of me let alone see anything else.

I heard the shuffling as my adversary moved towards me again. This time I was ready and aimed a powerful left hook-right hook combo (one of my favourites) at where I guessed my assailant to be. Both punches made satisfying contact with absolutely nothing and, as my momentum carried me forward, I received another blow to the stomach and a kick on the backside. The impact spun me around and I became reacquainted with the pile of rubbish that I had struggled up out of just a few seconds earlier.

This time I elected to stay down. I knew when I was beaten. The question was just how beaten was I going to become. I was also kind of worried. What kind of creature was I dealing with that could hit me so hard yet not be there when I hit back? Having been in more than one brawl in my time, I knew I wasn't that slow so I didn't think I could have missed my assailant.

I felt rather than saw the presence beside me as it bent down and grabbed me by the head with both hands. A voice whispered in my ear.

'Stay away from things that don't concern you,' it said in an accent I couldn't quite place but one that sounded vaguely familiar.

This just added to the mystery: a powerful creature that hit like a hammer, had a body that let punches pass through it, spoke like an extra out of a cheap '40s movie and had powerfully bad breath. I had to ask, of course.

'What kind of things?'

'Your new client and his missing ornament. It might be much healthier for you if you found another line of work in the short term.'

'Says who?' I was getting a little braver (and a lot more foolish).

'Says someone who thinks that you mightn't like hospital food and might prefer walking without the aid of hired help.'

I was now even more confused, as well as smelling like a cheap fruit and vegetable store. How had someone found out about my new client so quickly and, more to the point, why didn't they want me involved in the case? Before I could ask anything else the voice said, 'Remember our little conversation, otherwise I'll call again. Now it's time for sleepies. Nighty night.'

There was a firm tap to the top of my head by something hard, a bright explosion of light and then darkness as what was left of my faculties took command and wisely elected to shut everything down. Unconscious, I slumped to the ground.

3

On the Case

Two things struck me almost simultaneously when I woke up: the sky was incredibly blue and the only part of me that didn't actually hurt was my left elbow. My mind then went from neutral into first gear and started to tie the two thoughts together into a coherent concept. As I could see the sky, it meant I was lying on my back and the fact that I hurt all over was probably something to do with why I was lying on my back. Then the memory of the previous night's encounter sauntered casually into my head to force my brain into a higher gear. I'd been beaten to a pulp by an invisible someone who I couldn't touch, who had fists like mallets and knew about my current case. This was not a good start to the day and the prospect of another encounter with Gruff at my new client's residence meant it was only going to get worse.

I groaned as I hauled myself to my feet, shedding bits of cardboard, rotten food and used magic beans. I smelled like a garbage cocktail and figured that my new employer wouldn't take too kindly to my turning up at his residence in my present state. Like all good gumshoes, I always kept a spare suit at the office for those important occasions when I needed a one – like being roughed up, thrown in the river or being forced to spend the night sleeping in garbage. This was obviously one of those important occasions but after taking a step forward (very slowly, very carefully) and then collapsing back on the ground, I surmised I might be a while getting back to the office. I felt in my pockets for my cell phone, hoping to get Gloria to organise a cab. When I eventually found it, it was in a number of small and separate pieces. Obviously I wasn't the only thing roughed up the previous night.

As I tried to work out how exactly I was going to resolve this particular dilemma, I heard a noise behind me. I'd like to say I spun snappily around, fists ready for another fight, but I'd be lying. If I had to spin around it would probably have taken me the rest of the morning to do so.

'Hey Mr Pig,' said a boy's voice. 'Why are you covered in beans?'

I eventually managed to look around very slowly and very carefully. A boy of about nine, keeping a very safe distance away, was looking at me with interest. Presumably he didn't get to see a pig in a suit covered with garbage every day. He was dressed in faded jeans, sneakers and a white T-shirt with Hubbard's Cubbard (Grimmtown's latest music phenomenon) emblazoned loudly across the front.

'I fell,' I said, keeping it simple.

'So how did you get that black eye?' he asked. Great: a small nosey boy.

'Fell against those boxes there.' I pointed to the pile of flat cardboard that had been boxes before I fell on them.

'And the cut lip?' A small, nosey, perceptive boy.

'Banged off the wall.'

'And how did your clothes get torn?' Now he was becoming irritating on top of being small, nosey and perceptive.

'Look,' I said in exasperation. 'Shouldn't you be at school or out begging or something?'

'Nah,' he replied. 'I don't go to school on Saturdays.'

In my defence, I can only say that my deductive powers were still impaired as a result of the previous night's incident, otherwise, of course, I'd have worked that out in a matter of seconds. That's my excuse and I'm sticking to it.

He finally decided I was fairly harmless – or at least wasn't in a position to do him any real harm – and asked if I needed help. As his chances of carrying me were about the same as Dumbo falling out of the sky on us, I asked him to find a payphone and call Gloria.

'Tell her Harry needs a cab,' I groaned, throwing some coins and my business card at him. 'There should be a phone box out on the street somewhere.'

He looked at the card with great interest. 'Wow, a detective. How cool is that?'

'At the moment, not very,' I replied. 'Just make the call and I'll make it worth your while.'

'You mean I can work for you; be your informant or something?'

'No. I mean I'll give you ten bucks.'

His face dropped. 'But I hear all kinds of cool stuff. I could be really useful, specially with my contacts.'

'Look kid,' I said with as much patience as I could muster (which wasn't really a lot). 'If I need to know who stole the Queen of Heart's tarts I'll contact you, OK. Now can you just make the call? Please.'

He trudged down the alleyway to the street and I tried to clean up my clothes. Apart from used magic beans there were a number of wet newspapers, a variety of vegetables, an old bedspring and spaghetti on various parts of my person. I wasn't sure if I was removing them or smearing them in. When I was finished I certainly didn't smell any better and my suit would never be worn again thanks to the many non-removable stains it now sported. Moving very carefully and very painfully I made my way back towards the street, one aching step at a time.

To my surprise, the kid had made the call and a cab was waiting at the kerb for me. When the driver saw my condition (or smelled my condition, to be more accurate), he was understandably reluctant to let me into his cab. After looking in the back of it I didn't see how I could have made conditions there any worse as the back seat and floor were covered with candy wrappers, old newspapers, apple cores, melted chocolate and various strange and unsavoury-looking stains. If I hadn't known better I'd have assumed the cab had spent the night in the same pile of garbage as I had. When I pointed this out to the driver – and waved a twenty under his nose – he not-so-graciously consented to take me back to the office. As I was getting into the cab I reached into my pocket, drew out a ten-dollar note and handed it to the kid.

'Here kid,' I said. 'Thanks for your help. By the way, what's your name?'

'Jack,' he replied, examining the note for authenticity. 'Jack Horner.'

'Well, Jack Horner, maybe I'll see you around.'

'Count on it Mister.' He turned and walked back down the alleyway.

The cab pulled away and made its way back to my office. I wasn't in the mood for chat so after the cab driver had covered the usual in-taxi topics (weather, sport, vacations, weather again and traffic) without a hint of a response from me, he wisely chose to drive the rest of the journey in silence. At least I gave him a tip when we got to the office: I told him where he could find a good car cleaning service. He didn't seem too impressed as he drove off.

As I entered my office, Gloria tried (none too successfully) not to laugh.

'I shouldn't ask,' she giggled, 'but what happened to you? You look like you slept in garbage.'

I was about to point out how accurate she was and then decided not to give her the satisfaction. I have my pride, you know. With what was left of my dignity I slimed my way into my office. Within a matter of minutes I was clean, well, clean*er* at any rate, sartorially more elegant and, more importantly, smelling a lot less like rotten vegetables. That kind of thing can have a negative effect on clients and this was a client I didn't want to affect negatively, especially on my first day. I opened the top drawer of my desk and took out a spare phone. I had a running supply of spares; cell phones tended to have a limited life expectancy in my pockets. In fact, I suspected that the phone company had a special factory just making phones for me, such was the rate I went through them.

Gloria was still smirking when I came back out.

'That's a bit better, but not much,' she said. If anything, her smirk had gotten wider.

'Thanks for the beauty tips,' I replied. 'Maybe you should take it up professionally. You're obviously wasted in this job.'

'Now, now, I'm only trying to help.'

'Well, try harder.' I headed for the door and walked down to where my car was parked. Sliding into the driver's seat I gave myself a last once-over in the mirror.

'Presentable,' I murmured. 'Not at my best, but I should pass muster. At least they won't know that I spent the night sleeping in an alleyway.'

I started the car and drove uptown to see how the other half lived. Nestling in the foothills on the north side of town, Frog Prince Heights – possibly Grimmtown's most exclusive residential area – was home to the richest, most famous and probably most downright crooked of our citizens. Most of the very large and tasteless mansions had their own security service and enough electronic surveillance to make even the most paranoid of residents comfortable in their beds at night. As was the case with all residential areas of this type, the higher up the hills you went, the bigger the estates got. To my total lack of surprise, my client's home (if a word like home could do justice to the palace I drove up to) was right at the top of the hill overlooking the entire town.

'Master of all he surveys, no doubt,' I said, as I pulled up at the very large, very imposing and very closed gates that were embedded in even larger and more imposing walls. Just to the left of the gates was a small speaker underneath which was a bright red button. Pressing the button, I waited for a response. As I sat there, I imagined that very hidden, very small, very expensive and very-high-resolution cameras were even now trained on me, watching my every move. I didn't have to wait too long.

'Yes,' crackled a voice from the speaker.

'Harry Pigg. I have an appointment.'

'Just one moment.'

A please would have been nice, but I imagined detectives were as high in the food chain of visitors to the mansion as the mailman and the garbage collector so I figured manners weren't part of standard operating procedure.

The gates swung open very quietly and very quickly. I was a bit disappointed; I had imagined they'd be more imposing and ominous with lots of creaking and rattling.

The intercom crackled again. 'Drive through,' said the voice. 'Follow the road around to the side. You'll be met there.'

I followed the driveway up to the house, past lawns that looked as though they were manicured with nail scissors rather than mown. The house itself was a monument to bad taste or blind architects. Someone had clearly tried to incorporate my client's eastern origins into a gothic pile. It was as if a giant (and we have plenty in the locality) had dropped the Taj Mahal on Dracula's Castle and then cemented bits of Barad-dûr on afterwards for effect. Minarets jostled for space with pagodas, battlements and some downright ugly and bored-looking gargoyles. It hurt my eyes just to look at it, and I was wearing shades.

I drove around the side of this tasteless monstrosity to be greeted by another one. Waiting for me at what I presumed was the tradesman's entrance was an ogre, proudly displaying his 'Ogre Security – Not On Our Watch' badge. He was an imposing figure – all muscle and boils. Slowly he checked my ID before letting me out of the car. I could see his lips move as he read the details. The fact that he could actually read impressed me no end – most ogres I knew preferred to eat books rather than read them. Good roughage, apparently.

'So you weren't watching the other night, then?' I asked.

'Huh?' he replied.

I pointed to his badge.

'The other night?' I repeated. 'On your watch? Did you guys take the night off when the lamp was stolen?'

'What lamp?'

'Your boss's lamp. The one that...' Seeing the blank look on his face it was obvious that Ogre Security provided the muscle to keep the grounds free of intruders but didn't have too much input to the more sophisticated security inside the house. 'Never mind. Can I go in now?'

He even held the door open for me as I entered the house. A polite security guard, whatever next?

Inside, my good friend Gruff was waiting for me and, by the look on his face, wasn't relishing the job.

'Ah Mr Gruff, so good of you to meet me. I recognised your foul stench as soon as I came aboard. Showers broken, eh?'

He looked at me and I could tell he was struggling to come back with a witty reply, or indeed any reply. I smiled at his discomfort.

'Never mind,' I said. 'If you practise hard in front of a mirror maybe you'll learn to string more than two words together for the next time we meet. Wouldn't that be nice?'

He glowered as he led me through the house. It was just as tasteless on the inside as on the out. Furniture of various styles, shapes and sizes jostled for position with figurines, sculptures, assorted suits of exotic armour and a variety of plants. It looked like a storage depot for an antiques store run by a florist rather than a place someone actually lived in.

I was led through so many passages and rooms that I soon lost my way and had to depend on my guide to stop me from getting lost.

Eventually we arrived at a steel door that dominated the end of yet another long corridor. It was the kind of door that was more suited to the front of a large castle to keep invading hordes at bay rather than guarding a rich man's trinkets.

'The study,' said Gruff. 'I'll let you in once I've switched off the security system.'

He pressed some numbers on a keypad beside the door. There was a grinding noise and some sequential clunking as locks were deactivated. The door slowly slid into the wall. Lights in the room flickered on as we entered. If the rest of the house had been a monument to clutter, this room was a testament to minimalism. Apart from a large cylindrical black pedestal in the middle of the room, it was completely empty. There were no windows and the only door was the one we had just come through.

I walked towards the pedestal to have a look. It was a column of black marble that came up roughly to my chest. On top was a smaller display stand covered in black velvet, upon which, presumably, the lamp had stood. On closer inspection I could still see the imprint of the lamp's base in the cloth.

'So this is where the lamp was kept,' I said.

'Yes,' said a familiar voice behind me. 'Hi-tech security and surveillance systems and still it disappeared.'

Aladdin strode into the room and shook my trotter. 'Glad you could make it.'

'My pleasure. Exactly how hi-tech was the security here?' I asked.

'If you care to step back to the door, we can show you.'

We all walked back to the entrance and Aladdin turned to the goat.

'Mr Gruff, if you would be so kind.'

Gruff punched some more numbers on the keypad and the lights in the room dimmed again.

'Firstly,' began my employer/landlord, 'the floor is basically one giant pressure pad. Once the security system is switched on anything heavier than a spider running across the room will trigger the alarm. Observe.' Taking a very clean, very expensive and very unused silk handkerchief from his jacket pocket he lobbed it gently into the room. It floated slowly downwards and had hardly touched the floor when strident alarms rang all over the house.

'In addition,' he continued, as Gruff frantically pressed buttons to silence the ringing, 'there is a laser grid in the room which will detect anyone that might, for example, try to suspend themselves from the ceiling and lower themselves down to the pedestal.'

Another flourish of the arm, some more button-punching from Gruff and suddenly a bright red criss-cross of beams filled the room. It looked like a 3-D map of New York. A network of lasers covered every part of the space, wall to wall and floor to ceiling. Anything that might possibly get into the room certainly wouldn't get very far without breaking one of the beams. I didn't need the alarm to be triggered again to tell me that.

'Cameras?' I enquired.

'On the wall,' came the reply and he pointed to a lens that tracked back and forth across the room. 'It scans the room constantly and the output is monitored from our security centre, which you may visit shortly. The entire system is controlled via this keypad here.' He pointed to the unit on the wall. 'It is activated every night at ten and disabled again at seven each morning. All access is monitored and recorded. On the night of the... ah... disappearance none of the systems were deactivated, the cameras showed nothing else in the room and the lasers weren't triggered. It is most intriguing.'

Intriguing wasn't the word I'd have used; downright baffling was the phrase that came into my head, but I suspected Aladdin was trying to maintain an outward demeanour of cool in keeping with his image.

'Has the camera footage been examined?' I asked.

'Yes,' said Aladdin. 'But it didn't show anything. On one sweep the lamp was there, on the next it was gone.'

'Well, just to be on the safe side, I'd like to have a look. Maybe something was missed.'

From the snort of indignation behind me, I assumed Gruff didn't agree with my supposition. Good.

Aladdin led me to the security centre. The footage from the previous night was loaded by the guard on duty and the tape forwarded to when the lamp vanished. The camera scanned the room from left to right and the lamp was clearly on its pedestal. When it tracked back on its next sweep the lamp was just as clearly gone, as Aladdin had claimed.

'See,' said Gruff in a very superior tone, as if challenging me to find something he'd missed. 'Now you see it; now you don't. Any ideas?'

Not being one to refuse a challenge, I asked for the footage to be replayed and studied the screen carefully, trying to spot anything out of place. On the fifth or sixth repeat, I saw it.

'Stop,' I exclaimed and the security guard immediately paused the tape. 'Look there, right at the base of the smaller pedestal. See?' I pointed to a tiny flash of light that sparkled briefly and disappeared almost immediately afterwards. 'Any chance of getting that enhanced?'

The guard worked his voodoo and magnified the picture.

'What is it, Mr Pigg?' Aladdin's face was so close to the screen, he blocked everyone else's view. 'I can't seem to make it out.'

I moved him gently aside and examined the camera footage carefully.

'If I didn't know better, I'd say it was a micro camera, the kind they use in hospitals to have a poke around people's insides,' I said when I had the opportunity for a closer look.

'But what the hell is it doing inside the display stand? It's solid marble.'

I was obviously putting two and two together and getting four slightly faster than the others – although in Gruff's case I suspected that he was only able to get to three with great difficulty and the help of crayons. It seemed to me that if the thieves couldn't drop into the room or walk across it without setting off any alarms, there was only one other method of entry for any creative burglar – a method that demanded incredible technique and no small amount of nerve.

I looked at Aladdin. 'I think I need to have a closer look at the room,' I said.

'But of course,' replied Aladdin and we walked back to the study.

As Gruff deactivated the alarm system again I noticed something else.

'Hold it,' I said. 'Turn it on again.'

As the red beams criss-crossed the room again, I pointed to the pedestal. 'Notice how the beams don't actually cross the area where the lamp was? If the lamp was taken, it wouldn't set off the alarm.'

'That's a crock,' sneered Gruff. 'No one can actually get to the lamp without breaking a beam or standing on the floor. How do you think they entered the room – they teleported in?'

'Maybe they didn't,' I said. 'Disable the lasers again so I can have another look.'

Once the alarm was off I walked towards the pedestal. A glass dome that didn't look as if it had ever been touched, let alone lifted, covered the top of the pedestal and was firmly clamped to the base. I was obviously in top detecting mode today as, when I looked at the surface of the pedestal through the glass, I could see what looked like a few tiny grains of salt – almost invisible to the human eye; but then again, I'm not human.

'Can you disable the clamps on the glass and turn the lights on full please?' I asked.

More buttons were pressed, and the clamps disengaged loudly. The lights came up to full strength as, very carefully, I lifted the glass dome off and put it gently on the floor. As I examined the pedestal Aladdin came up behind me.

'What do you see?' he asked.

'I'm not sure,' I replied, as I leaned in towards the pedestal for a more detailed examination. 'It may be nothing but...'

I picked up some of the grains and put them on my tongue. They weren't salt; they were tiny grains of sand. I looked more closely at the pedestal. Ever so gently I pushed the velvet stand. It slid easily to one side, revealing a gaping hole underneath.

'What in the blazes is this?' exclaimed Aladdin.

'Clearly, when your thieves couldn't access the room from above or through the walls, they went under. They used the micro camera to check when the surveillance system on the wall was sweeping the room and stole the lamp when it was off-camera.'

'But who could have done this and where does the hole go?'

'I don't know who, but that's what you've employed me to find out,' I replied. 'As to the where, I don't know that yet, either, but I think I know someone who can help me work it out.'

4

It's Off to Work We Go!

'You mean you want me to climb down there to see where it goes? Cool.'

Jack Horner was clearly excited by his new Apprentice Gumshoe role as he gazed into the hole. As Tom Thumb was out of town on a small vacation (sorry!), he was my next and only other choice, seeing as the hole was too small to allow anyone else to climb into it. After assuring an understandably concerned mother that he would come to no harm, she had reluctantly allowed him to come with me.

'No heroics, Jack,' I told him. 'Just follow the tunnel until we can find out where it comes out.' I pointed to the equipment he was wearing. 'The rope is for safety, the torch will light your way and the little gadget on your belt is a tracker. We can follow you wherever you go. You can talk to us with this.' I handed him a walkie-talkie.

'Will there be monsters down there?' he asked.

'I doubt that very much,' I said, as I checked the rope one more time and lifted him up onto the pedestal. He seemed disappointed at my response.

'Ready?' I asked. He nodded in reply.

'OK then, here we go.'

He stood on the pedestal, looked into the hole again and prepared for his descent. Slowly, he made his way down until he was holding on to the edge by his fingertips. He glanced at me, nodded that he was ready and then let go. I took the strain and lowered him down carefully, as much to avoid any back injury on my part as for his own safety. It didn't take long for him to reach the bottom.

'There's a passage leading away but I don't see any daylight.' His voice came through clearly on my walkie-talkie. 'I'm walking along it now.'

'OK Jack,' I said. 'Follow it slowly but be careful.'

After a few minutes I could hear a strange noise on the walkie-talkie.

'Jack? Are you OK?'

'Yeah, why?'

'I'm hearing some odd noises on the walkie-talkie.'

'Oh, that's just me singing,' Jack replied. 'I do it sometimes to pass the time when I'm walking.'

'Uh, right.' Was this kid afraid of anything?

'I've come to a turn in the tunnel,' he said after a few more minutes. 'It bends to the left.'

From the signal on the tracker screen, he looked to be outside the house now.

'OK Jack,' I said. 'Keep going. Can you see daylight now?'

'Yeah,' he replied. 'The entrance is just up ahead.'

44

'Stop when you get there. We'll come to meet you.'

'Roger wilco. Over and out.' He'd obviously been watching too many war films.

Guided by Aladdin and Gruff, I walked back through the maze that was the inside of the house and made my way outside. As I walked across the lawn, I heard Jack's voice advising that he had reached the entrance to the tunnel. I told him to stick his head out and describe what he saw.

'It's a hole in the ground, surrounded by trees. I can hear cars so there must be a road nearby but I can't see it from where I'm standing.'

And, by extension, no one could see the hole from the road either.

I turned to Aladdin.

'From the signal, it looks as though the tunnel comes up just outside that wall there.' I pointed to the high wall running along the side of his estate. 'What's on the other side?'

Aladdin thought for a minute, and then for a few more. It was obvious he hadn't the faintest idea. He'd most likely never even noticed what was out there as he went in and out of his house every day – probably in a large limo with tinted windows.

I turned to Gruff. As chief of security I imagined he should know.

'It's a small open area between this house and the next. It's used occasionally by the local residents for walking their dogs, or at least those residents that, from time to time, actually venture out of their houses by means of their feet,' he said, glancing meaningfully at his boss. 'There are a few clumps of trees there. Most likely that's where your minion will be.'

We made our way out the main gate and along by those very imposing walls around Aladdin's house. It was easy to see why the thieves had gone under. The walls were very high with barbed wire on top and, as Gruff explained while we walked, equipped with more pressure sensors. If anything heavier than a sparrow landed on them, the alarms would go off. Even if an intruder was able to get over the walls without setting off the alarms (maybe he was a good pole-vaulter, I don't know) the grounds were full of heat sensors and more cameras. If he managed to get past those minor inconveniences, Ogre 'Not On Our Watch' Security would probably have fun using him as a volleyball. Your common or garden thief didn't stand a chance. It made me even more curious as to what type of thief I was dealing with.

We arrived at the open ground and could see Jack waving at us from a clump of trees about fifty feet from the wall.

'Over here,' he shouted.

When we got to him he was only too eager to show us where he had come out. We pushed through the trees with difficulty as they were very close together, and examined the tunnel. It looked like a very professional job: perfectly circular, level floor and smooth walls with supports to prevent accidental collapse. From its size, the diggers were also apparently quite small. I would have had problems had I been obliged to navigate it.

As I looked at the area around the tunnel entrance, something hanging off one of the branches caught my eye. Closer inspection revealed a bright green thread blowing gently in the wind. One of the thieves must have snagged an exceedingly loud item of clothing on the tree as he made his escape.

At this stage my brain, which, for obvious reasons, had understandably been functioning below par for most of the day, began to power itself up and began asking key questions (although not aloud). More to the point it also began to answer them. Perhaps my assailant wasn't quite as mysterious as I had thought. Putting the information about the tunnel together with the thread and my strange encounter of the previous night, a pattern began to emerge. I needed to get an expert opinion about tunnels and the creatures that dug them. It was time for a trip to the enchanted forest.

I turned to my client.

'Mr Aladdin,' I said. 'I believe, based on what we've just seen, that I am beginning to make some progress in the matter of your missing lamp. I need to make some calls and meet some people. I should have an update for you by tonight. May I contact you then?'

He whipped a card out of his inside pocket.

'My direct number; I am always available. Is there anything you'd care to share now?'

Of course there wasn't. All I had were a few ideas and a bizarre theory that was slowly taking shape but I wasn't going to tell him that.

'Not at this time. I will provide a full update later.'

He grunted, which I assumed was an acknowledgement, and we walked back to the house.

'Until later, then,' he said as Jack and I got into my car.

'Later,' I agreed and drove away. As the huge walls disappeared from view behind us, I told Jack where we were going.

'Are we really going into the enchanted forest?' he asked. 'I've never been.'

It should be pointed out right here that no self-respecting fairy tale town like ours would be without an enchanted forest. It was the location of choice for any laboratory, workshop or secret lair for magicians, wizards, warlocks, witches, alchemists, thaumaturges, vampires and the obligatory mad scientist. There is usually at least one mountain smack in the middle guarded by a horrible monster (usually a dragon) and reputed to be the location of a hoard of treasure.

If truth be known, however, most of the mountains were now just tourist attractions, the treasure having been plundered centuries before and the dragon killed in the process (and replaced by a very realistic animatronic duplicate to keep the punters happy). If you were looking for magic trees (of wood as opposed to those car air freshners that smell nice), cottages made of confectionery, any sword embedded in a stone, unofficial spell-casters, illegal potion sellers or two-headed birds, the enchanted forest was the place to go. Grimmtown's forest had an additional attraction for me, however, one that might go a long way towards solving this case.

We made our way back down from the lofty plateau of Frog Prince Heights, drove across town and into the forest. Fortunately, our destination wasn't too far in. There were far too many unpleasant things lying in wait deep in the forest for unsuspecting adventurers or unaccompanied tour parties and I had no urge to encounter any of them again (yes, I've been there before). After a short drive along a dark, tree-lined road, I pulled up to yet another large gate with yet another anonymous security system.

'The Heigh Ho Diamond Mining Company,' said Jack, reading the ornate sign over the gate. 'Why are we coming here?'

'Because if anyone can tell me anything about who built that tunnel,' I said, leaning out of the car to activate the speaker beside the gate, 'it's the chaps who run this place.'

'Name?' crackled a voice from the speaker. If I didn't know better, I'd swear it was the same voice as the one at Aladdin's.

'Just tell the lads it's Harry and I'd appreciate a moment of their time.'

Almost as soon as I'd finished speaking, the gates swung open – a lot slower and with a lot more gravitas than those at Aladdin's. There was no drive up to the building though; the offices were right beside the gate. There were seven parking spaces marked 'Director', all occupied by very fast, very sleek and very expensive cars. I was almost embarrassed to park my heap of junk beside them. Almost, but not quite – I'm unusually thick-skinned for a pig. We got out of the car and entered the office. As I opened the door, I turned to Jack.

'Not a word, kid,' I warned. 'Just let me do the talking. Some of these guys can be a bit difficult to deal with so stay shtum.'

'Yes sir,' said Jack, giving me a very official-looking salute that I hoped was tongue in cheek.

The reception area consisted of a few garish plastic chairs grouped around a battered coffee table, which was stacked with the inevitable dog-eared three-year-old magazines. Behind a desk and facing the entrance a sour-looking receptionist glowered at me, as if my arrival was a personal affront to him and had somehow ruined his day. Behind him, running the length of the wall, were seven portraits – one for each of the company's directors.

'Take a seat,' he snapped. 'One of the Seven will meet you shortly.'

'Who are "the Seven"?' whispered Jack, as we sat down. 'Are they some kind of secret society with blood oaths, strange passwords and funny handshakes?'

'Nah,' I replied nonchalantly, picking up a well-thumbed copy of Miner's Monthly. 'Nothing so mysterious. They're seven dwarves, all brothers, who set up a diamond mining company here years ago. It's been very profitable. They've cornered the diamond market locally. If anyone knows about digging tunnels, these guys do; they're experts in their chosen field – or under their chosen field even.'

Fortunately we weren't kept waiting too long. A door in the wall facing us opened and a large, red, bulbous nose appeared followed – it seemed like hours later – by the rest of the dwarf. Unfortunately it was Grumpy, my least favourite.

'Well Pigg, whaddya want?' he growled. His interpersonal skills tended to leave a lot to be desired – most noticeably anything remotely resembling good manners. As a rule his brothers tended not to let him do press conferences when they announced their yearly results.

I, of course, knew exactly which buttons to press.

'I'm looking for some assistance please, Mr...ah...it's Dopey, isn't it?' I replied, knowing full well how much it would aggravate him.

His nose turned even redder and the flush spread to the rest of his face. He glowered at me. 'It's Grumpy,' he said. 'G-R-U-M-P-Y!'

'By name and by nature,' I said under my breath to Jack. He looked down and I could see his cheeks bulge as he tried not to laugh. It's tough being a detective's assistant; you must maintain a calm demeanour at all times, especially when confronted with stressful situations.

He took up the magazine I'd been reading and developed an intense interest in an article on new methods of extracting metals from abandoned mines.

'Apologies, Mr Grumpy. I tend to confuse you and your brothers,' I lied. 'I'm looking for information about tunnels and those who dig them. As you have an undoubted expertise in this area, I figure that if anyone can help me it will be you.'

Flattery will obviously get you everywhere as Grumpy positively preened when he heard me compliment him. He puffed up his chest and strutted across the room. I could see his face gradually assume a less aggressive shade of red as he came towards me.

'What kind of information?' he asked.

I gave him the details of the tunnel I'd found without revealing where it had been dug or why. He considered what I'd said.

'Definitely made by experts from the sound of it, which does narrow it down. The best in the business are Little People. It's almost genetic with us. We have an affinity with stone; we love being underground and have an innate skill in burrowing, digging and making holes.'

'What kind of Little People are we talking about?' I asked.

'Well, apart from my brothers and me – and you know it isn't us,' he said, 'you've got other dwarves, who usually dig in rock; Halflings, who are good with earth, and fairies, good for small and very basic holes only and purely for sleeping in.'

I wasn't aware of any of these operating illegally in or around Grimmtown and neither was Mr Grumpy. As his company tended to employ all the expert diggers in the region, he would know of any newcomers – particularly as he would probably end up giving them a job, especially if they showed any kind of talent for tunnelling.

'Anyone else?' I asked.

'There are a few others that have shown tunnelling tendencies in the past. Kobolds, leprechauns, gnomes, the occasional Orc and, on very rare occasions, elves, although they've got soft hands so they tend to lotion a lot afterwards.'

I could tell he didn't hold elves in high esteem. I shared his opinion. They tended to stand around looking mysteriously into the middle distance declaiming loudly and pompously such phrases as 'The saucer is broken; milk will be spilled this night.' They never got invited to parties as they usually drank all the beer and, most annoyingly, never seemed to get drunk – apart from a tingling sensation in their fingers.

I figured that this was about as much information as I was going to get. It wasn't a lot but it did give me an inkling of where I should go next. I thanked Grumpy, dragged Jack away from his magazine and headed back to the car.

5

If You Go Down to the Woods Today

As I drove back through the forest I kept going over the events of the past two days. Things were starting to make a little sense – although not much. As I mulled over the case Jack nudged me in the side with a very bony elbow.

'Mr Pigg,' he said, 'don't look now, but I think we're being followed.'

'What makes you say that?' I asked.

'Well, the car behind us doesn't appear to have a driver and it's been tailing us since we left the dwarves' place.'

I looked in the mirror. He was right. Directly behind us was a very large, very black and very battered car with no driver obviously behind the wheel. As I looked it began to speed up. I could see the steering wheel rotate but it seemed to be doing so of its own accord. Maybe the Invisible Man was driving the car but, frankly, I doubted it – he had been advised to take taxis, as, every time he got behind the wheel, he tended to cause a small panic.

This was now getting beyond a joke and I wasn't the one who was laughing. Suddenly, the car accelerated again and rammed us from behind. The impact jolted us forward. Fortunately, apart from being winded, we didn't suffer any injuries, our seatbelts preventing any major harm.

'Whee!' shouted Jack. 'This is just like a roller coaster. Does this always happen when you drive?'

'No,' I said, trying to keep one eye on the road ahead and one on the car behind (not an easy task). 'Only on good days.'

Of course, car chases never take place on straight wide roads that run for miles with no sharp turns or oncoming traffic. Oh no, apparently convention dictates that they must take place through a busy metropolis with lots of hills, a narrow dirt track running along a sheer drop into the ocean or, as in my case, through a dark forest with a twisty road, lots of sharp bends and (being an enchanted forest) trees that might take exception to being woken up and take a swipe at whatever vehicle had done the waking. The bigger the tree, the more likely your car was to suddenly develop the art of flight when one of its branches made contact. Typically it wasn't the flying that one needed to be worried about; usually it was the landing – which tended to be uncontrolled, totally lacking in technique and, almost inevitably, resulted in your vehicle being embedded up to its rear doors in the ground. Most cars tended never to get back on the road after contact with one of our magic trees.

As I swerved to avoid hitting one of these trees and to try to ensure that my pursuer didn't, I had another of my really bright ideas.

'Hold tight,' I roared at Jack as I pressed hard on the accelerator. 'This could get scary.'

'You mean it gets better?' he shouted back, grinning from ear to ear. 'This is the coolest ride I've ever been on. Go Harry!' He stretched both arms up over his head, as people do just as they get their photograph taken on the scary part of a roller coaster ride, and yelled at the top of his voice. Truly this child had no fear.

The sudden burst of acceleration had, for a few seconds, taken me away from my pursuer. Rather than head towards the forest's edge, however, I took one of the trails deeper into the trees. I had a very specific destination in mind and one that might, if my timing was right, get this particular pursuer permanently off our backs.

As we drove further into the forest, the trees grew closer together and, eventually, their branches became so entwined over the road they formed a natural tunnel, shutting out daylight completely. I flicked on the headlights and they gave just enough illumination to prevent me driving off the road. On either side, gnarled branches were trying to grab at the car as we passed but I was going so fast they only scraped off the sides. They might be ruining the bodywork, but at least the bodies inside the car were undamaged – for now.

I recklessly navigated turn after turn (by the skin of my teeth in most cases), the road getting narrower and windier as we drove. I wasn't particularly scared of the forest; being chased by an invisible maniac tended to force all other thoughts of being frightened from one's mind. Our pursuer wasn't quite as reckless though, preferring to drive fast enough to keep us in his sights but not so fast as to spin off the road. We would hardly have been that lucky but that wasn't my main objective. It would, however, have made what I was about to do much less of a risk – especially to Jack and me – if he'd managed to hit something other than us in the interim.

A fork in the road came up so fast that, even though I was expecting it, I still nearly ploughed straight into the tree that stood right where the road split in two. I swung the steering wheel in an effort to keep the car on track. It screeched around the right-hand turn, leaving a liberal helping of rubber on the road. I was hoping my pursuer might not be so lucky but as I looked in the mirror I saw him take the fork a little less dramatically than I had and continue his relentless pursuit. We were now driving in total darkness such was the tree cover all around us. Even the car's headlamps didn't do much to light the way.

I was now driving purely on instinct. Bends came and went in a blur and all the while I could see the lights of the other car behind us, never closing the gap but never losing any ground either. Well, if things went according to plan, there would soon be a fair, and somewhat unexpected, distance between us. I turned to Jack.

'Hold on tight. Things might get a little bumpier.'

His face lit up like a searchlight. 'You mean it gets better?'

'Oh yeah, much better,' I replied grimly. 'Just make sure you're well strapped in.'

At last we were arriving at our destination. In front of us the road narrowed and curved around sharply to the left. Right on the bend stood a large and very old ash tree. Its gnarled branches hung down over the road, trailing long green strands of moss. As we approached they began to twitch as if anticipating our imminent arrival. I stood on the brakes and the car stopped abruptly just in front of the tree, jerking both of us forward. Moss draped across the windscreen, obscuring our visibility, but I was only interested in what I could see out of my side window. Jack was looking over his shoulder to see where our pursuer was and was finally starting to panic.

'Why have you stopped, Harry? He's getting closer.'

'I know. Just another few seconds.' I began to rev up the car.

'We don't have a few seconds. He's right on us.' Jack was really panicking now.

There was a blurred movement of something grey and gnarled coming towards us from the side and I instantly accelerated. The car shot forward as if it had been fired from a cannon. Our pursuer, who had sped into the space we'd just vacated, was suddenly swept sideways by a large and very fast moving branch. There was a loud wail from inside the car as it was catapulted across the road and smashed through the undergrowth on the opposite side, leaving a large and impressive vehicle-shaped hole in the bushes. Where the car had been on the road, a few leaves floated gently to the ground.

'Now that's what I call a flying car,' I muttered with satisfaction. 'James Bond, eat your heart out.'

Before I could take too much pleasure in the somewhat premature end to the chase, I had to drive my own car out of reach of the ash tree's branches before it had a second swipe. Better safe than even more damaged, I always say.

'Well, let's take a look at the incredible flying car,' I said, as I opened the door and got out. 'From the noise that it made as it flew through the air with the greatest of ease, I very much doubt that it was driverless.'

As Jack joined me and we began to make our way across to where the other car had landed I turned to the ash tree. 'Thanks Leslie,' I said. 'I can always depend on you to miss me.'

The tree shook its branches violently and sprayed moss in all directions.

'Maybe next time, Pigg,' it said in a voice that made Treebeard sound like a soprano. 'You can't be lucky forever.'

'What's his problem?' asked Jack.

'Some other time,' I replied. 'It's a long story. Suffice to say that, ever since my last encounter with him, he's had a deep longing to play baseball with me – using me as the ball.'

We made our way through the undergrowth. It wasn't too difficult as the flying car had cleared a wide path for us. We found it in a tree, jammed into the junction of two large branches. On the driver's side the door was open. Fortunately for me it was within climbing distance. Very carefully, I climbed up to the car and peered inside. Whoever – or whatever – had been driving had clearly done a runner, leaving nothing in the way of clues behind. Apart from the glass all over the floor, the inside of the car was spotlessly clean. I was now convinced that, despite initial appearances to the contrary, there had been a driver. Something had been screaming in terror as the car took flight and that same something had managed to open the door and disappear before we got there. All I had to do now was figure out what that something was, and if there's one thing I'm good at (actually, there are lots of things I'm good at) it's figuring things out. I hadn't actually expected to find anything in the car – that was a long shot. I was more interested in what may have been on the front. I swung around to the remains of the hood. Steam hissed from the mangled engine but there was no obvious smell of gasoline so I figured I was safe. I ran my trotters carefully over the front grille and felt something jammed in.

'Let's see what we've got here,' I muttered, pulling at the mysterious object.

There was a sudden screech of metal as the object I was investigating came off in my hand. With a loud shout, I fell back off the branch and plummeted to the ground. Fortunately for Jack I missed him when I landed. Unfortunately for me I also managed to miss anything remotely resembling a soft landing and hit the ground with a very unsatisfactory (from my viewpoint, at any rate) thud. As I groaned in pain and checked all extremities for damage for the second time in a day, I swore I could hear the ash tree sniggering in tones so low I could feel my fillings vibrate. He was obviously enjoying a minor victory at my expense. As I'm not a petty pig – but more because there was a small boy in the vicinity – I refrained from making an obscene gesture at him, although someone had once pointed out to me that it was very hard to make obscene gestures when you didn't have any fingers.

I was, by now, mastering the art of getting gingerly to my trotters so I managed it much better this time. Once I had dusted off the leaves and other debris, I examined the object, the removal of which had caused me to fall in the first place.

'What is it, Harry?' asked Jack.

'Exactly what I'd expected,' I replied. 'It's a very small but very powerful camera.'

'What was it doing on the front of the car?'

'Well, think of it like this, if you were really small and had to drive a car, how would you be able to see where you were going if you couldn't see over the front dash?'

I had now dismissed the idea of being beaten up by an invisible superhero. All the evidence I'd gathered during the course of the day had led me to a different, less super and far more irritating solution. The camera had now confirmed my suspicions. I now needed to pay a visit to someone very annoying. This someone would not appreciate me visiting him, so, in order to prevent a recurrence of the previous night's unfortunate incident, I needed some additional protection.

'OK Jack, let's head back to the ranch. There's nothing more to see here.'

As we walked back to the car, being very careful to avoid any aggressive branches, I reached for my shiny new phone and made a quick call. For my next trick I would definitely require a very specific type of assistance, and I knew exactly who could provide it.

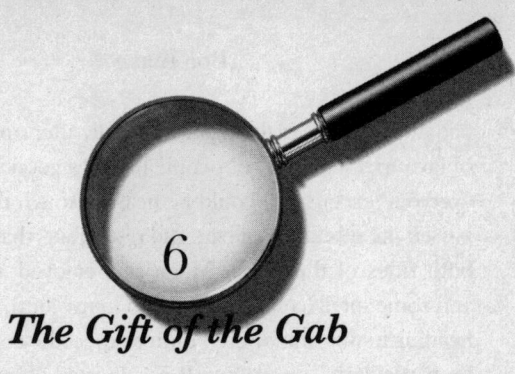

6

The Gift of the Gab

It was early evening when we got back into town. After dropping Jack at home with a promise I'd call him again if I needed him, I drove back to the office, parked the car and headed back towards the main street. After the previous night's experience I kept a regular look over both shoulders and avoided any dark, or even not that brightly lit, alleyways. If there weren't at least twenty people in the same street as me then it wasn't going to be one I was going to walk down, across or through. Once bitten – or once punched, threatened and deposited in garbage – had made me very careful and I was also concerned about the impact that constantly being decorated with rotten vegetables was having on my laundry bill – not to mention my personal grooming.

After navigating the side streets of Grimmtown without attracting any undue attention, I turned onto Hans Christian Andersen Street. Dusk had made way for night and the city's bright young things were all out in their vampire-look finery again. On every corner a girl from Little Matchgirls Inc. was hawking hot dogs, burgers and fried chicken – the company had diversified over the years, especially after smoking fell out of favour. The sound of people having a good time (at least, everyone except me) could be heard through the doors as I passed the multitude of bars and restaurants that proliferated both sides of the street. Much as I enjoyed a quiet drink and some intellectual conversation in my local, the bar I was heading to was one where I didn't expect the conversation to be particularly stimulating. It was located about halfway up the street and had a particularly distinctive frontage – it was bright green. Outside the Blarney Tone, Grimmtown's only Irish bar ('Come for the Music, You'll Stay for the Craic'), a very small man in a very shiny bright green and white costume was exhorting passers-by to come in and enjoy the fun inside. Benny was a gnome and Grimmtown's worst leprechaun impersonator. I stopped behind him to listen to his patter. He had the worst Irish accent I'd ever heard; yes, even worse than Tom Cruise's in Far and Away – and I should know, my grandfather was prime Irish bacon.

'Ah sure now, will ye not come in and try a Guinness. 'Tis only the best in the town, brought in specially, direct from the brewery in Dublin. There's a free plate of crubeens thrown in for good measure. You won't see the like anywhere else.' As he spoke he did a little jig that caused the rather large silver buckles on his black shoes to clang like a set of enormous bells.

The rest of his outfit was just as subtle as his shoes. Bright white socks stretched up to just below the knees, where they were met by bright green plus fours that were kept up by a large black belt. White frills that seemed to explode from a shirt so white it hurt to look at it fronted an equally lurid green jacket. An obviously fake ginger beard and curly wig covered most of his grey-skinned face like a bright orange fungus. On his head he wore a long black hat with yet another shiny buckle. It looked like someone had rammed a bucket upside-down on his head.

He was possibly the least convincing leprechaun in history but he was also just the man I needed to talk to. Despite the ludicrous outfit he was very sturdily built. In fact, he was the type of guy who could deliver a hefty punch to your midriff while, owing to his size, every attempt you made to hit him back just went over his head.

He still hadn't noticed me as I approached him carefully and tapped him on the shoulder.

'Evening Benny,' I said cheerfully.

He spun around and for a split second his face dropped as he recognised me. Like the true pro he vainly aspired to be, he immediately recovered and began his Irish shtick again but his first reaction had given him away.

'Begorrah Mr Pigg, is it yourself that's in it. And out on a fine night like this too. Sure why not drop in and try a pint of the black stuff. 'Tis the best in town.' As he spoke he made to move towards me. This time I was somewhat better prepared and, as I quickly stepped back, I nodded to two large shapes that had just as quickly, but a lot more silently, moved up behind him. As he tried to land a punch on me a large hand grabbed his neck from behind and suddenly jerked him backwards and upwards. He dangled in mid-air, legs kicking so fast he looked like he was pedalling an invisible bicycle. The hand held his head level with my eyes and squeezed ever so slightly. Benny's face began to turn an interesting shade of bright red as his neck began to constrict under the pressure.

'Now, Benny,' I said cheerfully, 'perhaps we can discuss your recent forays into robbery and GBH.'

'I... don't... know... what... you... mean,' he managed to choke out. By now his face was turning from red to purple and I watched with fascination (and no small degree of pleasure I must shamefully admit).

'Ah, but how remiss of me,' I said. 'I'm forgetting my manners. Before we start, allow me to introduce my colleagues, Mr Lewis and Mr Carroll. They're ogres.' Considering their size, strength and skin colour it was probably stating the obvious, but I wanted to see Benny sweat and show him that I meant business. My 'colleagues' were each over eight feet tall with skin that almost matched Benny's jacket in hue. Their impressively muscular frames were barely contained by the immaculate evening suits they had squeezed into. They were definitely the type of guys (or creatures) that you needed when there was a possibility of any unpleasantness, as they tended to be a very effective deterrent – as they were now proving.

'Now that the introductions are over, perhaps we can get down to business,' I said to Benny. 'Let me put some perspective on this for you, just in case you're confused.'

As Benny wasn't the sharpest tack in the box I figured I'd better spell it out for him. Before I could start, however, I noticed that his face was now bright blue. Perhaps the ogres were being a trifle too eager.

'Mr Lewis, perhaps a little less pressure.'

Lewis grunted and relaxed his hand slightly. Benny's face returned to its previous shade of purple.

'OK, Benny,' I said, 'let's begin. Once upon a time there was a gnome named Benny. Not too bright but always on the lookout for an opportunity, he made a living as a dodgy leprechaun impersonator trying to get gullible customers into the local Irish bar. And, by the way, you need to work on that accent. Are you with me so far?'

He nodded, his head barely moving.

'Good. Now, our friend Benny probably got an offer from someone to help him acquire a valuable antique from a local businessman. It certainly wasn't Benny's idea, what with him not being too bright and all, but the offer was impressive enough to encourage him. How am I doing so far?'

Benny gave another little nod.

'This is called detecting, Benny. It's what I do. I examine the clues and determine what's going on. This then allows me to follow a specific line of inquiry. This specific line of inquiry has, most fortuitously, brought me to you.

'In this instance, your mysterious client clearly needed someone with some subterranean delving skills and who would also do what he was told, no questions asked, as long as the price was right.

'Unfortunately he picked you,' I continued. 'You may be a great digger, which of course pointed me in the right direction, but you were a trifle careless at the scene of the crime.' I reached into my pocket and removed a small envelope. Inside was the green thread I'd found on the tree outside Aladdin's. 'You appear to have picked up a minor tear on your sleeve and, look, the thread I happen to have here matches almost perfectly. What a coincidence, eh?'

There was another gurgle that could have meant anything from 'What great detective work. You've certainly rumbled me. I confess' to 'I'm slowly choking to death here, could you ask your moron to reduce the pressure on my neck somewhat.'

I chose to interpret it as the latter, although I certainly wouldn't describe Lewis as a moron – at least not to his face. Another nod and Lewis eased his grip slightly more.

'Now I know that you aren't working alone, not only because you haven't got the smarts to pull this off on your own, but even you couldn't drive a car into the enchanted forest, crash it rather spectacularly and then get back here to play little green man with the tourists so quickly. Nice trick by the way, getting one of your idiot cronies to use the camera to see where he was going because he was too small to look over

the wheel. I take it you didn't come up with that idea either?'
The response was another faint shake of the head.

'Now I know that, as a rule, when goblins get together,
rather than the total being greater than the sum of the parts,
the collective IQ tends drop to well below that of the dumbest
member – a kind of anti-synergy. I suspect, therefore, that
you were the mere executors of this cunning plan that, in all
likelihood, was probably written out in very small words and
very short sentences so you and your cronies could follow it
without screwing up – which you failed miserably to do. So
here's what I'm going to do.' I looked Benny straight in the
eye to let him know that I still meant business. 'I'm going
to instruct Mr Lewis here to let you go. When he does so
you will make no attempt to do anything other than answer
whatever questions I may put to you. Should you attempt to
assault either of the ogres (which would be rather foolish)
or me or even try to make a break for it, the only break you
will experience will be a random assortment of your limbs.
Understood?'

Benny nodded ever so slightly. I looked at Lewis and he
dropped the goblin with such force that he lay on the ground
groaning pitifully. I nudged him with my shoe.

'C'mon Benny, up you get. If you need some help you
only have to ask. Either Mr Lewis or Mr Carroll will be only
too delighted to assist you.'

This suggestion seemed to give Benny some incentive as
he struggled to his feet slowly and, I have to add, with a lot

less style than I had shown previously. Maybe he just didn't have as much practice at getting up as me.

'OK, Benny, your starter for ten: where's the lamp?'

Benny looked up at me with an expression that would have made his mother clutch him to her chest and console him with lots of 'there, theres'. Fortunately for both of us I wasn't his mother so he didn't get the sympathy vote from me. He also spared me the 'what lamp?' routine, presumably as even he could figure out exactly how much I already knew and that I wasn't prepared to tolerate being messed around any more – or maybe it was just the large and very obvious presence of my two companions. Despite this, however, his reply was only marginally more helpful (which wasn't saying a lot).

'I don't have it,' he gasped.

'Not a good answer, Benny,' I said. 'I'd have thought that by now you'd realise there is no point in playing dumb – or, in your case, even more dumb than usual – with us. We're really not in the mood.'

'No, really, I don't have it. Honest.' From the fearful look on his face I suspected that he was finally telling the truth. Now all I had to do was find out what he had done with the lamp, get it back to Aladdin, pocket a large pay packet and wallow in the satisfaction of a job well done. Smiling with anticipation, I asked the obvious question again and received a not-so-obvious answer that wiped the smirk off my face and plummeted me even deeper into the murk that was Grimmtown's underworld.

'One last time, where's the lamp, Benny?'

'Edna has it,' he answered.

I looked at him, dumbfounded. 'Edna?' I repeated.

He nodded his head gingerly. 'Edna,' he said with more conviction.

'Edna, as in Edna?'

He nodded again. 'Yep, that's her.'

'Please tell me you're joking and this is just another idiotic attempt to throw me off the track,' I begged, but I knew Benny was telling the truth, I just didn't want to believe it. I just wanted him to suddenly spring to his feet and yell, 'Gotcha! I had it in me rucksack all the time.' I knew this wouldn't happen. Quite apart from the fact that he could barely stand anyway, his entire demeanour suggested he was being truthful – and without being coerced any further, either.

If Edna was involved, I needed to tread very carefully indeed. In actual fact I needed to run very quickly in the opposite direction if I wished to retain the use of all my limbs. This was more like a Harry Pigg case: lots of different people vying to be the next to hurt me in new and interesting ways while I manfully (or pigfully) tried to represent my client to the best of my ability (and he was one of those people threatening to hurt me). I figured I'd get whatever information Benny hadn't yet imparted and then decide whether it would be more advisable to get the next bus out of town or stay and get beaten up at least one more time.

'OK Benny, let's take it from the top – and don't leave anything out.'

7

In the White Room

'Emerald Isle of Adventure? Are you serious?'
Benny nodded glumly. 'Emerald Isle of Adventure,'
he repeated. Repetition tended to happen a lot
when you talked to Benny. It helped him focus.

'You really were going to call the theme park that?' This
beggared belief. I knew Benny was as dumb as a bucket of
shrimp, I just didn't realise the extent of his stupidity. This
master plan of his plumbed new depths of imbecility.

Benny and his 'Brains' Trust' of gnomish friends had
decided that, with the proliferation of successful and highly
profitable theme parks based on our illustrious history that
had sprung up all around Grimmtown, it might be a rather
splendid idea to develop one based around Ireland and its
past, him and his buddies being leprechaun impersonators
and all. 'A sure fire hit' was how he'd described it. So far I
had been regaled with how it would include Finn McCool's
Rollercoaster of Terror, the Lucky Leprechaun Log Flume
and the Find the Crock o' Gold Hall of Mirrors. When you
eventually grew tired of all the excitement you could then

relax in Mother Ireland's Bacon and Cabbage Emporium with a nice Guinness.

Now I like my thrills as much as the next man – except in this case seeing as the next man was Benny – but I just didn't think this particular wonderland had the necessary pizzazz. In fact, if it managed to draw more than twenty gullible tourists on the day it opened (if it ever did), I'd eat my own head.

To cut a long, very rambling and disjointed story short (and to spare you many tedious digressions, pauses and nonsensical musings, because I know even your patience would wear very thin), Benny had put an ad in the local press describing the concept and seeking investors for this sure-fire hit. To his – and no one else's – surprise, the take-up on the proposal was less than stellar but, just as he was about to abandon his plan, he received an email (and yes the address was evilgenius@criminalmasterminds.com) promising him a very large investment in the scheme in return for a very small favour. This favour (and I'm sure *you* can see what's coming, even if Benny couldn't) involved Benny and the boys using their burrowing skills to recover an artifact that had allegedly been stolen from this mysterious benefactor many years previously. The story was embellished by references to family heirlooms, dastardly thieves, a poor granny pining for her long lost lamp and, of course, the dangling of the incentive of part of the investment up front with the rest to follow upon successful delivery of the lamp. Benny had swallowed it hook, line, sinker, fishing rod and angler.

The down payment had arrived and Benny had acquired the lamp – which considering his track record had to qualify as a spectacular success. All he then had to do was deliver it and the Emerald Isle of Adventure would be a reality. As you can imagine, the delivery hadn't gone according to plan – hardly surprising when you consider who the delivery boys were.

Benny and his band of idiots had begun making their way to the drop-off point. If the sight of a band of gnomes trying to look furtive while walking through the busiest part of town dressed in lurid green outfits didn't grab attention, the same group babbling on loudly about how they were going to spend their newly-acquired fortune surely would. Unfortunately for them, it grabbed the attention of two of Edna's henchmen.

Now I need to digress slightly here, as I'm sure you're asking, 'Who is Edna?' and 'Why does she want to divest those poor unfortunate gnomes of their one chance of a happy ending?' The answer to the second question is easy once you understand the first. Edna is one of a group of four witches who basically run all of Grimmtown's organised crime – a kind of Mezzo-sopranos or Contraltos, if you will. They've unofficially divided the town up into four districts and Edna runs the West Side – hence her title: the Wicked Witch of the West Side. Their control of all criminal activity is total. Nothing illegal moves without them knowing about it or profiting from it to some extent. They are a family I had kept well clear of over the years and I had no wish to alter that status any time soon. If, however, Edna did have the lamp, then that was a wish that was evidently about to come true, despite my best efforts to the contrary.

'So,' I said to Benny, 'to summarise the plan: there you were, a band of gnomes heading to a drop-off point in the middle of town, babbling on heedlessly about how you were going to be fabulously rich once you passed the lamp over to your mysterious benefactor, a lamp, incidentally, which one of you was actually carrying in a bright red shopping bag. Where in this cunning strategy do you think the obvious flaw was?'

Benny dropped his head in a semblance of shame and chose not to answer.

'So. On your way to the drop-off point – ah, where was this place, anyway?' I asked.

'Litter bin on the south corner of Wilde Park,' mumbled Benny.

'Of course it was. Instead of somewhere quiet and secluded, you picked one of the busiest intersections in the city. Could you have been any more obvious?' I laughed. Benny's story was becoming more nonsensical by the minute.

'So, as I say, you were on your way to the drop-off point when someone from Edna's gang grabbed the bag. Now, what I can't figure out is this: you guys are thick but can certainly pack a punch.' I rubbed my stomach at the memory of just how packed the punch was. 'How come they got the lamp so easily?'

Benny mumbled again.

'Speak up, Benny,' I asked. 'I can't make out a word you're saying.'

'Otto took it,' said Benny, a little more articulate this time. 'He just flew down out of nowhere, grabbed the bag in his claws and scrammed again.'

Otto the Owl was one of Edna's henchbirds and I suppose that a bright red bag wasn't too hard to miss if you had spent your formative years flying around a forest hunting tiny rodents in total darkness.

To put it mildly, this new development presented me with a problem: my client's lamp was now in the possession of one of Grimmtown's most ruthless criminal families; a family who would have no compunction about rearranging my anatomy should I even hint that it might be a good idea for them to return it. My client would also, in all likelihood, rearrange my anatomy if I failed to return his lamp – and probably evict me to boot. Either way it seemed that anatomy rearranging was about to become my newest pastime and one I didn't particularly feel like taking up, especially as we were talking about my anatomy and its capacity to be rearranged. In the faint hope that I might get something else out of him, I turned back to Benny.

'Apart from emails,' I asked, 'I don't suppose you ever got to meet this investor of yours?'

'Not as such, no,' Benny said. 'But I came close one night or, at least, I think I did.'

'What do you mean?'

'Well, the night we were due to receive our down payment my instructions were to go into the men's rest room in the Blarney Tone, make sure I was alone, send a text message to a particular number that I was ready, and wait for further instructions. When I got in there, I waited until it was empty, did as I was asked and stood there. Suddenly there was a loud bang, everything went white and next thing I knew I was in a room with funny walls, lots of rugs and carpets and stuff like that. I couldn't see anyone in the room but a voice told me to pick up a bag that was on a table beside me. As soon as I did, I was suddenly back in the rest room again with my down payment.' He looked at me. 'I know how it sounds, but it's the truth, Mr Pigg. Honest.'

I was just about to tell him how ludicrous his story was and did he really expect me to swallow something so ridiculous when there was a loud bang, everything went white and I was suddenly in a room with funny walls, lots of rugs and carpets and stuff like that.

As you can imagine, it took a few seconds to get my bearings seeing as I had suddenly been transported from Point A to Point B without any knowledge of where Point B actually was, how far it was from Point A, or exactly how precarious my situation now was as a result. At first glance, fortunately, precarious didn't seem to figure high on the agenda. I was in a long oval-shaped room with no windows or obvious doors. Bright white walls curved inwards from an equally white floor to an oval ceiling. Lamps ran along the walls illuminating the room with a soothing white light. It was, in fact, a very white room.

The only sop to an alternative colour scheme were the very expensive-looking rugs (expensive to my unsophisticated eyes at any rate) that were casually flung on the floor in a feng-shui kind of way and the colourful tapestries that hung from the walls. The décor suggested the Orient, which, considering my current assignment, hardly seemed like a coincidence. Whoever had summoned me here was clearly connected to Aladdin in some way – if only by culture. My suspicion, however, based on Benny's tale was that I was in the presence of his mysterious stranger, although the room was currently devoid of any presence other than me. As most of the people I'd encountered in this case so far seemed intent on doing me harm, this was a small mercy for which I was incredibly thankful.

As I stood there I became aware of a faint whirring behind me. I turned around – ever so slowly – to see if some strange mechanical torture device was about to dismember me. To my relief, I found myself gazing at a not-so-sinister, large and very hi-tech-looking computer. There were so many wires, cables and other devices hanging from it, it looked like it was in an intensive care unit. With all the printers, modems, scanners, microphones and assorted paraphernalia – that even I couldn't figure out the use of – there seemed to be enough hardware to run a small country and still have enough processing power for a quick game of Half-Life while affairs of state were being mulled over.

It also occurred to me that the computer might shed some light on the identity of the thief and maybe even some clue as to their motive. As I surreptitiously reached for the keyboard a voice erupted from the walls around the room.

'Naughty, naughty, Mr Pigg,' it boomed. 'Please step away from my machine.'

I raised my trotters over my head and took three steps back from the hardware. Looking around, I tried to see where the voice was coming from. Best I could figure was that there were speakers hidden behind the wall hangings and, from the quality of the sound, they were clearly very expensive.

'Please forgive both my brusque manner and the somewhat unorthodox kidnapping,' the voice continued. 'I hadn't meant for us to meet in quite these circumstances. In fact, I hadn't intended for us to meet at all but I suspect that my original choice of miners left much to be desired when it came to not leaving obvious, or indeed any, clues behind. Clearly I should have been more discriminating in my selection.'

'If you pay peanuts, you get monkeys,' I said. I enjoy a cliché every now and again and it was the only thing I could come up with while I tried to figure out what to do next.

I'm not always witty and quick with the rapier-like repartee – hard, as I'm sure it is, for you to believe.

'Indeed,' said the voice. 'And while you're trying, no doubt, to figure out where you are, who I am and what you should do next, allow me to recommend that you make yourself comfortable while I make some suggestions.'

I slowly sank onto a very ornate and very comfortable ottoman and waited.

'As you have probably already deduced, the gnomes were clearly not a good investment. In less than twenty-four hours they stole the lamp but left clues so blatant that a corpse could have followed them. They then managed, with an incredible lack of subtlety, to make Grimmtown's organised crime fraternity aware that they had an object of immense value and then, while bringing it to me, succeeded in handing it over to one of our more illustrious criminal masterminds in the process. Do I summarise the situation accurately?'

I nodded weakly as I could see where this was going and I didn't need a map to give me directions.

'I think I now need to utilise the resources of a more accomplished craftsman to reacquire the lamp and you will probably not be surprised when I tell you that I have chosen you, Mr Pigg.'

I opened my mouth to object with whatever reasons I could think of but before I could even come up with 'Scintillating Excuse Number One to Avoid Locating a Stolen Lamp', I was interrupted.

'I will, of course, not tolerate any refusal on your part,' said the voice with an uncanny sense of anticipation. 'My need for this lamp is far greater than your need to refuse and I can change you into anything I choose should you prove to be difficult.'

Now I was getting paranoid. There was a definite trend here and it wasn't one I was particularly enamoured with. Why was everyone suddenly so intent on hiring me and, when I expressed any kind of reluctance, quite prepared to use very effective threats of bodily harm to compel me to agree to work for them? Was I really that good, or was I just that unlucky? Was it possible for anyone to be that unlucky? Maybe I just had that kind of face.

Whatever the reason, it now looked like I had two clients, both of whom wanted the same thing and one of them was now telling me I had to steal back an already stolen lamp from one of our most ruthless criminals or face an unpleasant, but as yet undefined, alternative. With my imagination, however, I could think of quite a few 'alternatives', none of which were remotely attractive and none of which I particularly wanted to face. It looked like I was about to add breaking and entering to my already extensive set of skills.

'OK,' I said, resigning myself to the inevitable. 'What do I have to do?'

The whirring sound increased in volume and a large amount of paper was ejected from one of the printers at the high-tech end of the room. From what I could see, it was building plans of some kind.

'Blueprints of Madame Edna's building,' confirmed the voice. 'My understanding is that the lamp is in a room on the third floor, securely under lock and key. Unfortunately, security in the building is, by definition, rather tight. This means, of course, that it will be difficult to find a means of access that won't be guarded in some way. I, however, have a high degree of confidence that, if undetected access can be found, then you are just the pig to find it. I would suggest that, if you are successful, you should reflect on the options available to you and, perhaps, the recovery of the lamp may not be as difficult as it first appears.'

Great, now he was talking in riddles as well. I grabbed the sheaf of papers and looked at the ceiling.

'In the off chance that I do manage to get the lamp back, how do I contact you again?'

'You don't,' came the reply. 'I shall contact you.'

'Great,' I said, with a considerable lack of enthusiasm. 'Can I go now?'

There was another loud bang and associated white light. When my head cleared I found myself back outside the Blarney Tone, staring into Benny's ugly mug. As Messrs Lewis and Carroll were still in close proximity it mitigated against his taking advantage of my disorientation. When asked, they confirmed that I had disappeared from right in front of their eyes, had been absent for about ten minutes, and then reappeared in exactly the same spot.

This had been one of the strangest days of my life and I should know; I've had quite a few. I decided it was time to cut my losses and plan for tomorrow before things got any weirder.

I turned to Benny. 'Benny, stick to the day job and give up burglary.' I paused for a moment and reconsidered. 'On second thoughts give up the day job as well. You suck at it. And while we're on the subject, please don't ever let me see you within a mile of me, or my associates here may play with your neck again.'

Benny went pale but nodded in agreement.

'Very good, Benny; you're a quick study.'

He disappeared up the street so fast I was impressed with his powers of recovery.

Satisfied that they were no longer required, Lewis and Carroll disappeared back into the darkness.

Clutching the plans I'd been given, I trudged slowly home to formulate some way that would allow me to enter Edna's base of operations, steal back the lamp from under her very prominent witch's nose, escape undetected and return it to one of its alleged owners, while trying to keep the other alleged owner from doing something unpleasant to me.

Easy!

8

A Brief Interlude in which Harry Doesn't Get Threatened or Beaten up by Anyone

In the relative safety of my apartment I finally managed to find some time to consider the case.

None of it seemed to make any sense. The original theft was clearly an inside job because of the in-depth knowledge of the security systems, but I didn't figure either of the two possible suspects (Gruff or Aladdin) for it. Aladdin had no obvious need to steal his own lamp and was wealthy enough to suggest that an insurance scam wasn't high on his list of priorities. Gruff seemed to be too loyal to his employer to consider stealing the lamp and was probably only too aware of the likely consequences if he was found to have been responsible. There was nobody else in Aladdin's employ that had either the smarts or the access, so where did that leave me?

Well, I'd (sort of) met someone who claimed to have masterminded the job even if I didn't have the faintest idea who he was either. He seemed to fall into the criminal megalomaniac category Boy Blue had referred to, as he had all the tricks of the trade: deep dramatic voice, an impressive HQ – at least what I saw of it – and a strong desire to show off. All he needed to complete the effect was a white Persian cat to sit in his lap and be petted constantly – assuming he actually had a lap.

Mind you, having used Benny as the actual thief also demonstrated a certain fallibility on his part. Maybe he wasn't as all-powerful as he thought. Of course, he was powerful enough to compel me into reacquiring the lamp for him – a task I had to take somewhat seriously or suffer embarrassing, if not downright unpleasant, consequences.

Heaving a sigh of such resignation that it would have evoked sympathy from a zombie, I resigned myself to my lot, rolled out the plans and studied them as best I could. I didn't know how Mr Big (I know, I know, tremendously clichéd but I couldn't keep calling him by the more pretentious and even more unoriginal 'mysterious stranger' moniker now, could I?) had gotten the plans but they were incredibly detailed. Were there any premises in Grimmtown he didn't have an in-depth knowledge of?

The plans, however, confirmed what I had already suspected: all access to Edna's residence was controlled by yet more sophisticated and, no doubt, very effective security systems. Complementing these were somewhat less sophisticated – but no less effective – guards who were, in all probability, armed with a variety of interesting instruments of pain. The only way I was going in the front door was as the main ingredient in a Chinese takeaway – and that was a step that I was, understandably, very reluctant to take.

The more I studied the plans, the more unlikely the prospect of recovering the lamp became. I could see no way in that avoided me being detected and if I couldn't get in then my career as Grimmtown's foremost detective would come to a premature end.

I was about to ball the plans up and fling them in the garbage when I noticed a small tunnel I hadn't seen before. At first glance, it looked like it led into one of the lower levels of the house from under the street. Upon closer examination, it became clear that it didn't lead into the house as such. Rather, its primary function was to take some unpleasant material away from the house. Yes, you've guessed it; if I was to successfully enter the house undetected, I was going to have to do it via the sewage outlet. Yet another lucky break for me, eh? And if I actually managed to get into the building, I still had to navigate my way to where the lamp was kept, find some way of taking it and make my way back out again – all without alerting anybody. No problem!

Ah well, may as well be hung for a boar as for a piglet. All it needed was a little bit of careful preparation, a massive slice of good luck, no one to flush suddenly and I might yet get out of this smelling of roses (or possibly not, bearing in mind what I was going to have to crawl through).

I reached for the phone as, once more, I was going to have to utilise the resources of another of my many contacts – and I was well connected. There may have been a thinness on the ground when it came to my informants but, when I needed to lay my hands on 'stuff', I knew some people who knew some people who could source anything: from doorknobs to a tactical nuclear warhead.

Ezekiel Clubfoote was the man to go to for all your gumshoe shopping requirements. If he didn't have it, or couldn't get his hands on it, then chances were it didn't exist or you never really needed it in the first place. He had been an exceedingly poor shoemaker (from both a finance and quality perspective) some years back. Business had, consequently, been pretty bad but, on the brink of total ruin, he had allegedly made some deal with elves that rescued his career. Apparently, whatever raw material he left in the shop at close of business each day would have been transformed into high quality footwear by the next morning. Suddenly his shoes and, by extension, his services were in popular demand and in Grimmtown being in popular demand made you a very wealthy person indeed.

Not one to miss an opportunity, he experimented with leaving other materials out for the elves each night. No matter what he left out, the next morning he'd be presented with a finished product of some description. Put out some clay – get high-class porcelain. Leave some wood: an antique chair. From such small beginnings are large warehouses of equipment - and a thriving distribution company - made.

I dialled and waited. I didn't have to wait long.

'Yes?' came a very cultured voice from the other end of the phone.

'Zeke, it's Harry. I need something from your elves.'

'Of course you do. Big or small?'

'Not too big this time; I only need a lock pick, a wetsuit and an Orc costume.'

Considering the last time I had contacted him, I had looked for infrared glasses, four kangaroos, a machete and a rocket launcher (remind me to tell you sometime), a lock pick wasn't too excessive a demand.

'An Orc costume?' I imagined his eyes opening wide in surprise. 'There isn't really any such thing. It's more of a collection of smelly furs and skins held together by dirt and an occasional chain. You don't so much acquire one as have bits of one stick to you after rolling around in a rubbish tip.'

Considering what happened during my initial encounter with Benny, I knew what he meant.

'And what kind of lock will you be picking? And, no, I don't want to know the personal details - just the technical ones,' said Zeke.

'Well, there's the problem,' I replied. 'You see, I'm not really sure. I suspect that the door I have to open will more than likely be locked, but I have no idea how sophisticated this lock may be.'

'Hmmm, without knowing the details, I suspect that you'll need the Masterblaster. It's so good, a man, or indeed a pig, with no fingers could open any lock with it. It's a "Choice of the Month" in Lock Pickers Illustrated and it doesn't come more highly recommended that that, let me tell you.'

I rolled my eyes upwards. He did so like his little sales pitches.

'Fine, fine. How soon can I have them?'

'Give me an hour. I need to make sure it's in my next run so I'll organise to have them dropped off to you as soon as I get them.'

'Thanks, Zeke. I owe you.'

'Yes, you do. And I'll collect.' Zeke hung up, leaving me with the dial tone for company.

While I waited for the equipment, I studied the plans some more. Edna's outlet (if you'll forgive the phrase) connected to a main sewer that serviced the entire block where her headquarters was located. Access to this larger sewer could be gained via a number of manholes; I just needed to find one that wasn't too public and just far enough away to avoid being seen by whatever surveillance systems she had in operation. Mind you, that was the easy part. After that I had to make my way up a very narrow tunnel and hope that the exit at the other end was a little larger than a U-bend.

In the short term, personal hygiene would be a thing of the past and a shower very much an aspirational goal until I had what I came for – assuming I managed to get that far in the first place.

I can't say I was particularly looking forward to the next few hours.

9

Flushed with Success

Of course, no matter how well I plan these jobs, there's always something. Well, have you ever tried to open a manhole using trotters? Let me tell you, it's not easy. For one thing, it's hard to get a grip on the rim. For another, manhole covers are heavy and, thirdly, I was on my own. Lastly, I was wearing a bright blue wetsuit (although it was so worn and full of holes it could be more accurately described as a dampsuit) under a foul-smelling collection of rags that could probably have represented the height of fashion from an Orc's perspective. All this, and I had to try not to appear too conspicuous as well. As a result, by the time I finally got the drain open (with the help of a tyre iron), my wetsuit had even more holes, my back hurt, and my skin was a darker shade of pink than usual from my exertions.

As I levered the manhole cover off, I lost my grip on it but, thanks to my quick reflexes and uncanny sense of self-preservation, I didn't lose any body parts as it fell heavily (and with a very loud clang) to the ground. Fortunately, as

Edna's stronghold was in an area where the occasional loud noise wasn't an undue cause for concern, it didn't appear to have attracted any attention.

I shone my torch down the manhole and looked in carefully. At first glance, the sewers didn't look (or smell) too unpleasant. In actual fact they smelled better than me. This, I suspected, was largely because of the recent heavy rains, which had run off via storm drains and into the sewage system, effectively washing most of the unpleasant stuff away.

Now that was something to be thankful for.

Grabbing the top rung of a metal ladder that led from the street down into the sewers, I slowly and carefully made my descent. Arriving safely at the bottom I took my bearings with the help of the plans.

I was in a large tunnel that stretched off into the darkness in both directions. Smaller tunnels opened out from the walls as far as I could see but none, I was glad to note, seemed to be active. The only evidence of any discharge other than rainwater from these tunnels was a trail of green scum that dripped downwards towards the floor of the main sewer. Although I was ankle deep in liquid, it appeared to be mostly water. Then again, I had no intention of examining it too closely. What I didn't know, wouldn't hurt me.

I had a quick look at the plans, figured I had to go right and slowly made my way up the tunnel trying to keep the sloshing to a minimum – just in case. Although I wasn't entirely sure which of the smaller outlets led into Edna's HQ, it didn't take me long to figure it out. Not surprisingly, it was the one with the large securely-padlocked grille that covered the entire tunnel entrance. After a few pulls it was evident that this grille wasn't going to come away from the wall that easily.

'OK Harry,' I said to myself as I reached for the lock pick. 'Let's see how good the Masterblaster is.'

In fairness, I haven't had much cause to pick locks in the past. Any time I've had to 'enter' a residence without legally coming in via the front door, I've found that the old credit card trick so beloved of TV detectives actually worked. It was, therefore, no surprise that jiggling little iron pins in a keyhole wasn't quite as simple as it first appeared. No matter how I tweaked, twisted and pulled at the lock, it stubbornly refused to open. Even reverting to Plan B – swearing at the grille – didn't appear to have any effect either.

In total frustration I hit out at the lock with my torch. To my surprise the lock broke and fell to the ground in pieces. Years of rust and an application of brute strength had succeeded where subtlety and bad language had failed.

Of course, it wouldn't be a Harry Pigg case without something bad happening as well. In this instance, the breaking of the lock had also resulted in the unfortunate breaking of the torch. I now had to navigate my way through a sewage outlet and into Edna's lair in total darkness, using only my sense of touch (and possibly smell).

I felt for the grille and dragged it away from the entrance. Aware that I was now possibly within earshot of one of Edna's more alert henchbeasts, I struggled to keep it from falling to the ground – which I managed to do at the expense of a large tear in my wetsuit and a pulled muscle in my shoulder. As if my job wasn't difficult enough already!

At least I was able to use the bars of the grille as a mini-ladder to lift myself into the smaller outlet. My shoulder objected strongly to being forced to help in dragging me up and into the tunnel but I managed to pull myself up without doing any additional damage.

This new tunnel was a tight squeeze and I was forced to crawl along, rubbing against the walls and roof as I did so. It was much narrower, much smellier and showed very distinct signs of much more frequent usage. Unpleasant substances stuck to my back and legs and I had no great urge to investigate what they actually were. In an effort to take my mind off my current situation, I pictured myself in a hot shower liberally applying sweet-smelling soap to my body. This seemed to work and I was wallowing in the imaginary sensation until my reverie was broken by a gurgling noise from somewhere up ahead.

'Oh no,' I said anxiously. 'Please don't let it be someone flushing. Anything but that.'

The gurgling grew noisier and it was joined by a loud flowing sound as something large and liquid made its way down towards me.

Frantically, I tried to reverse back down but in my panic I only succeeded in wedging myself tightly into the tunnel. Firmly stuck and unable to move, I could only close my eyes and mouth as a noxious brown liquid washed over (and under and around) me, covering me liberally in a foul-smelling residue.

Coughing and spluttering (and now smelling even worse than before), I tried to wipe my face clean but only succeeded in spreading the vile substance around even more. As there was no point in going back now, I slowly twisted and turned until I had forced myself free and gradually made my way up the tunnel again. Some things just shouldn't happen to a hard-working detective and getting liberally covered in raw sewage was most certainly one of them.

As I crawled slowly forward I saw a thin crack of light shining faintly through the roof ahead. Eager for any way of getting out of the tunnel, I struggled on. To my intense relief, the light came from where the side of a square metal drain cover wasn't flush (no pun intended) to the edge of a manhole. Hoping that I could push the cover off, I wedged my back underneath it and pushed upwards with all that was left of my strength. Slowly but surely it lifted away and slid off my back gently onto the floor above.

Muscles howling in pain, I hauled myself up and carefully peered over the edge. I was looking at a dimly lit corridor. From the dust on the floor, it wasn't one that was used too often so, thankful for one lucky break, I heaved myself out of the sewer and lay on the ground panting heavily, stretching my knotted muscles and trying to get my breath back. Now all I had to do was find the room where the lamp was kept, if the plans were to be believed, and steal it back.

I took the building plans from inside my wetsuit where I had stored them for safekeeping. Although stained with sweat and effluent they had escaped the worst of the deluge so I was able to work out where I was without too much difficulty.

If I was reading the plans correctly, I appeared to be in a basement. I just needed to make my way to the stairs at the end of the passageway, go up four levels, find the room halfway down a long corridor and take the lamp. Of course, I had no idea exactly how well protected the room was but at least I now knew how to get there. Limping slightly, smelling heavily of unmentionable substances and groaning as quietly as I could, I struggled towards the stairs.

If walking caused some discomfort then climbing the stairs was an exercise in agony. Every step upwards jarred another aching limb or my torn muscle. I felt as though I'd been skinned and roasted over a roaring fire. Everything burned or stung in some respect after my tunnel experience and, with my luck, there was no obvious hope of easing this agony in the near future.

When I eventually dragged myself to the top of the stairs, all I wanted to do was lie down and be mothered. As there wasn't a mother to be seen in the vicinity and as lying down would probably result in me not getting back up again for probably quite a few months, I willed myself to go on and through the door.

Fortunately, the door wasn't locked, as I probably wouldn't have been able to bend down to try my luck at another lock-picking attempt. Opening the door slightly as quietly as I could, I peered down the corridor. It looked more used than the one I'd just left but there didn't appear to be anyone on guard that I could see. Pushing the door open just enough to squeeze through I squelched carefully down the corridor towards the next flight of stairs.

I managed to climb three flights before meeting anyone. On the third floor landing two henchOrcs were standing guard. Now the reason for my cunning disguise could be revealed. Most of Edna's troops were Orcs – not too smart and not too alert but very handy in a fight. Looking like them, although a trifle larger, I might be able to make my way around the building without being too obvious.

I was about to find out how convincing my costume was. Keeping my head down, I shuffled towards the guards. As I got close, they recoiled at the smell. Good, at least they wouldn't look too closely. It also appeared as though I actually smelled worse than they did – which in itself was quite an achievement and something that, in other circumstances, I might have taken some (but not a lot of) pride in.

I knew some very basic Orcish – which to all intents and purposes sounds like a flu-ridden gorilla strangling a hyena – so when they hailed me I muttered something along the lines of being required on the third floor in order to relieve a sentry there. At least that's what I think I said; I could have just as easily asked the sentries for some hot, buttered toast and a glass of dragon's blood. Sometimes it was difficult to get those choking sounds just right. I must have been convincing (or smelly) enough, as they let me pass without examining me too carefully. Can't say I blame them. If I had been on sentry duty, I wouldn't have been too eager to examine me either.

I made my way up another, and hopefully last, flight of stairs. At the top I paused for breath and to give my long-suffering body some respite. A long corridor, covered in a luxurious red carpet, stretched out in front of me. Suits of armour lined the corridor, one beside each door. With one exception, all the doors were made of very ornate patterned wood. The exception was the door behind which, presumably, all Edna's interesting stuff was kept.

I walked up to it. It looked like a standard metal security door: grey, impregnable and securely locked. Heaving yet another of my many sighs of resignation, I took the lock pick from my pocket, cleaned it as best I could and began to jiggle the levers in the keyhole.

After ten minutes or so it had become clear that I was never going to add breaking and entering to my long list of skills. My efforts to pick the lock had resulted in very sore trotters, a rising sense of frustration and a door that steadfastly refused to be unlocked. Maybe I was doing something wrong or maybe it was just that the Masterblaster wasn't actually the state-of-the-art tool I had been promised. In any event, I suspected that hitting the door with whatever implement was to hand wouldn't be quite as successful as it had been down in the sewer. As I sweated and struggled, I became aware of a conversation from behind the door.

'How's he doing?' said a rough-sounding male voice.

'Not too good,' came the reply. 'He's been out there for a quite a while now and he still hasn't managed it.'

'How long do you think we should give him?' said the first voice again.

'I dunno,' replied the second. 'But I know I'm getting bored just waiting here. The fun is going out of it.'

'Let's not wait any more,' said the first voice again. 'Let's just do it now.'

'OK. On a count of three: one... two... three.'

Before I had a chance to make any kind of sense of the conversation, the door swung open and two pairs of hands reached out and grabbed me. Hauling me into the room, they threw me unceremoniously to the floor where I lay panting, aching, smelling and trying to get my bearings.

'Well, paint my backside green and call me a goblin,' said a loud and very familiar voice from right in front of me. 'If it isn't Harry Pigg, crap detective and failed burglar. I don't think I've ever seen anyone take so long to pick a lock. What kept you?'

My eyes ran slowly up past two legs so fat they were doing GBH to a pair of green stretch trousers. They traversed a torso that suggested its owner enjoyed several square meals a day (quite possibly a few circular, triangular and oval ones as well) and up to a face that defined new levels of ugliness, even for a witch. Imagine Jabba the Hutt with bright red lipstick and a long off-blonde straggly wig and you may get some idea of just how repulsive Edna – for it was she – actually was.

She grinned at me, which was a particularly unpleasant experience as it showed off a mouth with teeth that varied in shades of yellow and green, and that gave off a breath so unpleasant that I almost smelled good in comparison.

'There I was, wondering exactly what was so special about that lamp I took from Benny when suddenly you appear, stinking to high heaven and apparently eager to take it back.' She looked me straight in the eye – or at least as straight as someone whose eyeballs rotated in two different directions could – and leaned forward so our faces were almost touching. 'Looks like you're the man who can answer this most intriguing of questions. What a timely arrival, eh?'

She was about to slap me enthusiastically on the shoulder but quickly reconsidered when she saw what I was coated in.

She turned to the two henchOrcs who had dragged me into the room. They were small but very mean-looking.

'Tie him to a chair and hose him down,' she ordered. 'I'm not asking him questions until he smells better than he does now.'

She walked towards the door and, as she opened it, she appeared to have an afterthought.

'Oh and I'm going for a bath, boys,' she said with a malicious gleam in the eye that was currently looking at me. 'So no need to use up all the hot water on him, is there?' And with a long, loud and unpleasantly mocking laugh, she left the room.

10

Anyone for Pizza?

As you can imagine, it doesn't take too long for two very burly henchOrcs to tie a relatively defenceless pig securely to a chair – even a pig that they had to keep at arm's length owing to the smell. And there was going to be none of that slowly working the trotters free while being interrogated either. These guys were pros in the tying-up game. My trotters had been tied to each other, then to my body and then to the chair. I felt my extremities begin to go numb as the ropes constricted the flow of blood. The only way I was going to free myself was by diligent use of a chainsaw and there didn't appear to be one conveniently to hand. I had been trussed up more securely than Hannibal Lecter; all I was missing was the hockey mask.

While the goons located a long hose and began running it out of the room and down to the nearest bathroom, I took the opportunity to have a closer look at my surroundings. As I expected, bearing in mind what had just happened to me, the lamp was nowhere to be seen. The room itself was relatively bare. All it contained were a few chairs, a long table and what looked like a drinks cabinet. Considering where Aladdin had kept the lamp, this room was a bit of a surprise. I had expected more hi-tech surveillance and security systems.

A large oval mirror hung from the wall directly opposite me (presumably deliberately, so I could see just how bad I looked). Without going into too much detail, my skin was no longer a fetching shade of pink and the new coloration wasn't entirely due to bruising. What was left of my Orc costume was sodden and covered in a variety of strange substances that didn't warrant a more detailed forensic examination.

It looked as though whoever had supplied the plans to Mr Big had led him up the garden path (and into the garden shed whereupon they had hit him across the back of the head with a shovel), as there certainly wasn't any sign of a lamp here.

Even I couldn't figure out how to rescue myself from this particular predicament. Apart from the unpleasant experience of being hosed down with cold water, I also had the pleasure of Edna's interrogation to look forward to – and I was assuming this was going to be a little bit more intense than just having a bright light shone in my eyes while she shouted 'you will answer the questions' at me.

I was still looking around the room when the Orcs came back in. From the expression on their faces, it appeared as though they were relishing the thought of hosing me down. Can't say I blamed them; I was looking forward to a shower myself – albeit a somewhat hotter one than the one I was about to receive.

Grinning at each other, the two henchOrcs lifted the hose, aimed it at me and began to twist the nozzle. I turned away to shield my face and braced myself for the freezing deluge. There was silence, then two loud clangs in quick succession and the sound of the nozzle hitting the ground. After another brief pause this was followed by two more thuds – this time slightly further apart and much heavier. More importantly, I didn't seem to be getting wet.

I looked around very slowly and not without some trepidation as I had no idea what had just happened. To my utter amazement, both Orcs were lying unconscious on the ground. Standing over them, wielding a large metal leg – presumably borrowed from one of the suits of armour outside – was a very satisfied-looking Jack Horner.

'Jack,' I asked, somewhat stunned at this unexpected turn of events, 'what are you doing here?'

'Hey Mr Pigg,' he said cheerfully, 'I'm rescuing you. I told you you'd need my help.'

'But how did you find me?' I asked weakly.

'C'mon Mr Pigg,' he replied. 'You smell very strongly of shi... I mean poo. How difficult do you think it was to find you? I just had to follow my nose. Anyway, you left a trail of muddy footprints all over the building. It was easy.'

'And you got in how exactly?'

'Almost as easy. After I followed you here, I just bought

a pizza from the takeaway around the corner, stuck a red hat on my head, called to the front door and said I was delivering a super pepperoni to Grazgkh. There's always a Grazgkh around, it's the Orc version of Joe.'

And I was supposed to be the detective!

'Then I just made my way up through the building, following your trail,' he continued, obviously enjoying himself. 'These Orcs aren't too observant, are they? Not one noticed me all the way up. Then I crept up behind those two guys and hit them over the head with this leg.' He swung it around with some relish. 'They were so busy with the hose they never heard me.'

'Good work, Jack,' I said. 'Now, can you untie me and we can get the hell out of here before someone discovers I've escaped.'

'Righty-o,' he replied and went behind me to untangle the spaghetti of knots that bound me to the chair.

After a few minutes I still hadn't noticed any relieving flow of blood coursing back into my numb trotters.

'How are things going back there, Jack?' I asked.

'Not too good, Mr Pigg,' Jack replied. 'I can't seem to get these knots undone.'

'Well, try to find something that you can use to cut the ropes,' I said, scanning the room for anything that might have a sharp edge. 'But hurry. I'm sure Edna will be back soon, suitably refreshed, smelling very nice and eager to inflict pain.'

Jack began searching the room frantically, shifting bits of furniture aside as he looked for anything that might be used to set me free. As he searched I struggled to loosen the knots but my efforts were as fruitless as his. I could see that he was beginning to panic so I tried to calm him down.

'Take it easy, Jack. You need to calm down and focus. There must be something here we can use.'

'But I can't see anything, Mr Pigg.'

As I looked around the room yet again, I caught my reflection in the mirror. Inspiration struck me – and it was probably the only thing that had struck me recently that hadn't hurt me in some form or another.

'Jack,' I said urgently. 'Take that thing you hit the goblins with and throw it at the mirror. Cover your eyes as you do.'

After a moment's incomprehension, Jack suddenly understood and, grabbing the metal leg, he flung it at his reflection. There was a loud crash and shards of glass flew in all directions. When the noise died down, Jack slowly brought his arm away from his eyes and scanned the floor for a suitable piece of glass. He picked up a shard so big and sharp it looked like it could have beheaded an elephant and, with great care, began sawing at the ropes. As they began to fall to the ground, I could hear what sounded like a small army pounding across the floor overhead. Someone (or lots of someones) was coming to investigate the noise and I really didn't fancy being here when they arrived.

'Come on, Jack,' I muttered. 'Speed it up, speed it up.'

'I'm going as fast as I can,' he replied, panting from the effort. 'I don't want to cut my hands.'

'Cut hands will be the least of your worries if we don't get out of here soon.' As I spoke, the ropes binding my trotters fell to the floor. Despite the pain as the blood rushed back in, I grabbed the glass off Jack and attacked the other ropes binding me. The sharp edge cut cleanly through them and I stood up – a little bit unsteady but ready to accelerate out of the room as fast as I could.

'Good work, Jack. Now let's not be here.' I grabbed his hand and pulled him towards the door. As we were halfway across the room he stopped unexpectedly, almost pulling me off balance. I turned to him. He was looking at the broken mirror in fascination.

'Jack, what are you doing? We don't have time for admiring our reflections.' I was on the point of lifting him onto my shoulders and carrying him out when I saw what he was looking at. What he had broken wasn't a mirror; it was a door cleverly disguised as a mirror. With the glass surface now all over the floor we could see into the room beyond and sitting on a shelf (along with what I suspected was a lot of very expensive and probably very stolen artifacts) was what looked like Aladdin's lamp. It certainly looked battered enough.

'Nice one, Jack, I take it back. Get to the door and tell me when the ravening hordes charge down the corridor. If I'm quick enough we may be able to grab the lamp before they get here.'

Jack peered cautiously around the door.

'Nothing out there yet,' he reported, 'but there's definitely someone coming. I can hear lots of grunting, stomping and shouting. Hurry up.'

Very cautiously, so as not to cut myself on the jagged edges that were still embedded in the rim, I sidled through the doorway and into the storeroom beyond. Not even pausing to look at what other goodies might be on the shelves, I grabbed the lamp, stuffed it into my wetsuit and reversed just as carefully back out again. Once I was safely back out of the storeroom, I ran out the door, dragging Jack by the scruff of the neck as I went. Together we ran back down the corridor towards the stairs. As we did so, a horde of Orcs brandishing an interesting array of sharp and pointy objects came around the corner at the opposite end. Immediately spotting us (not that it was too difficult) they roared angrily and gave chase.

Fortunately for us, there were so many of them and the corridor was so narrow that they fell over each other in their eagerness to catch us. This slowed them down enough that we were able to get to the stairs. The two Orcs that manned the guard post on the landing tried to block our way but my impetus, speed and bulk bowled them easily aside and they tumbled down the stairs in front of us.

Tucking Jack under one arm, I threw a leg over the banister and slid down, trying to maintain what was a very precarious balance. For once, Jack didn't treat it as a theme park ride; presumably he was as scared as I was. The banister itself spiralled down in wide arcs all the way to the ground floor so I had no hairpin bends to navigate, which was probably just as well because with the rate we were accelerating, any sudden departure from the stairs would probably have resulted in us splattering against the wall at the far side of the room. Spotting a number of Orcs running up the stairs towards us I yelled at Jack to hold out his metal leg (which he'd shown the good foresight to hold on to) and he cut a swathe through them as we passed, their bodies cascading down the stairs like ugly skittles.

We reached the ground floor and flew off the end of the banister. Fortunately, the thick carpet broke our fall and we avoided a collision with any of the furniture. Dizzy but otherwise unhurt, we staggered to our feet and ran through the door to the basement. Grabbing the leg from Jack, I placed one end on the ground and wedged the other under the door handle. It wasn't going to hold our pursuers at bay for long but might give us enough of a lead to enable us to get to the drain safely.

As we charged recklessly down another flight of stairs there was a very satisfactory thump as the first of our pursuers hit the door, followed by more thumps and much shouting as the rest of the pack hit it (and the leading Orcs) with equal force.

'Quickly, Jack, let's go,' I urged. 'It won't hold them up for long.'

Jack nodded and picked up speed. Now he was beginning to leave me behind. Willing my body to one last effort, I caught up with him and we ran for the manhole. As we reached it, there was a loud splintering from behind us as the door finally gave way. We only had minutes before the Orcs reached us. Grabbing Jack, I threw him into the tunnel and dropped down behind him.

'Go, go, go,' I roared.

Jack disappeared down the tunnel and I followed as fast as I could. Thankfully, someone – most probably Edna – had taken a bath since my last passage through the drain, as it wasn't quite as unpleasant as previously, making our progress relatively more comfortable than before. In front of me, Jack was sliding away down the tunnel and I tried pigfully to keep up with him. Behind me I could hear voices raised in argument as the Orcs decided whether or not to follow us.

'You go first,' said one.

'Me? I'm not going in there,' said another in reply.

'Ma'am will be very angry.'

'Well you go, then.'

'I'll go if you go first.'

As is usual with Orcs in these situations, they then started squabbling and this soon erupted into a fully blown brawl. Orcs are good like that – low attention spans but high animosity. By the time we reached the main sewer, they'd probably have either all killed each other or forgotten all about who they were chasing in the first place. We made our way through the water back to the ladder and climbed up to the street.

As we headed back to the car, it struck me that Edna would be somewhat miffed that I had stolen back the lamp. She would be probably even more annoyed that she hadn't had the chance to slap me around a bit. I figured it wouldn't take her too long to track me down – especially as both my apartment and office were in the phone book.

I was going to have to come up with a plan to resolve this dilemma and this had to be the plan to beat all plans. In fact, this one had to be a doozy or I was quite possibly going to end up revisiting the sewers – this time face down and probably not breathing.

11

I Have a Cunning Plan!

With Jack safely dropped off home, I decided to lie low to try to avoid detection by all the various factions that were by now, presumably, scouring the town for me – and that didn't come any lower than the Humpty Inn chain of hotels. It was the cheapest and least reputable hotel chain in town. If they were any seedier you could have used them to feed birds. Fortunately, their very seediness meant that they were the perfect place to hide out as no one noticed, or even cared about, who was in the rooms.

Comfort wasn't high on the list of facilities offered by the hotel. The bed felt like it was made of rocks, there was a strange fungus growing on one of the walls and, yes, the room was lit up by the garish purple light from the neon sign that ran vertically along the front of the building and flashed on and off at regular intervals. The curtains didn't do much to block this light out as they looked to be made out of tissue paper.

The room had one very important feature, however – a working bathroom. Despite the imminent threat to my person, the first order of business was a long, hot, luxurious shower. I have to say I wallowed. If someone had broken in and pointed a gun at me, I'd have told them to get on with it and died a happy pig. Of such little pleasures is life made.

After my shower, and smelling a lot better, I sat at the wobbly dresser and studied the lamp carefully. It was as battered as its photograph suggested. The amount of dents in the metal suggested it had had a long and interesting history – quite a bit of which seemed to involve it being used as a football. It was so tarnished it was hard to make out what its original colour was. Try as I might, I couldn't open the lid. Although it didn't look to be sealed shut in any way, it just would not lift. I tried using a knife but it wouldn't budge. It was one stubborn lid.

There were no markings of any type on the surface, or at least none that I could see. I did contemplate dropping it in a fire to see if the flames revealed any mysterious writings but I didn't actually have a fireplace and I figured that a match wouldn't be quite as effective. In all probability, the room was so flammable even lighting a match would have caused it to catch fire.

I put the lamp on the dresser and stared at it. Then I stared at it some more and, just as I was about to give up, I stared at it especially hard. It didn't make any difference; it still sat there mocking me with its dullness and downright shabbiness.

Then I had a really outrageous idea: what if I rubbed it? What was there to lose? There was certainly a lot to gain, assuming the rumours were true. If all went according to legend then I was on the point of leaving all my troubles behind. Wealth beyond my wildest dreams was within my grasp. No more worries; no more Aladdin, mysterious stranger or Edna. And that could be a real result rather than just a turn of phrase.

The more I thought about it, the more it appealed to me. What could possibly go wrong? I figured that the more I thought about it the more likely I was to talk myself out of it. Best be decisive and take immediate action.

I grabbed the lamp with my left trotter. It wasn't easy but I managed it. Holding it level with my eyes I contemplated it one last time; it was still as dingy and battered as before. I slowly raised my right arm and, taking a deep breath, I brought the lamp towards my trotter and when they touched, I rubbed the surface furiously.

There was a... well... nothing actually. No sudden clap of thunder. No flash of light. No puff of smoke. No intimidating eastern gentleman with a trail of vapour where his lower legs should be. No deep and terrifying voice shouting: 'I am the Genie of the Lamp. What are your wishes, my Lord?'

Nothing!

The lamp still sat there silently mocking both my efforts and me. Either that or it wasn't as highly positioned on the alchemical plane as had previously been speculated. With a grunt, I flung it back on the dresser and headed for the bed. As I prepared for what looked like a very uncomfortable night's sleep, I took one last look back. Something about the shape of the lamp tried to trigger a thought at the back of my mind. My mind, however, was refusing to play ball and the door marked 'Free Association' stayed resolutely shut. In the off chance that my subconscious would do what my waking mind couldn't, I stumbled into the bed, pulled the flimsy blankets over me and was asleep in seconds.

I was also awake within seconds as the synapses in my brain – that had steadfastly refused to work earlier – set off a chain reaction that jolted me back to full consciousness. I sat bolt upright in the bed with a large grin on my face.

'You are so clever,' I shouted gleefully. 'No wonder you wanted to steal the lamp. If it was me, I'd probably have done the same. Any wonder it didn't work when I rubbed it.'

The beginnings of a really dastardly plan began to form in my mind as I tried to figure out where the nearest Internet café was. As I dressed, I thought I heard a noise from the corridor outside my room. I padded carefully to the door and put my ear against the wood. Fortunately, the quality of the workmanship was as poor as everything else in the hotel. The door was so thin I could hear clearly what was happening on the other side. As per usual, it didn't bode well for me.

'Is this the room?' whispered a voice – very low and very guttural; very Orcish, in fact.

'Yeah, he only checked in an hour ago,' replied a second voice I recognised as the concierge from downstairs. So much for anonymity. Obviously Edna's grapevine was very efficient. Once he'd heard she was looking for a pig, it didn't take the concierge too long to make both the obvious connection and the inevitable phone call and no doubt pocket the reward.

As I was only seconds from having a horde of Orcs explode into my room I had to think very fast. I grabbed the dresser and pulled it in front of the door. It wouldn't be a barricade – more a minor hindrance – but it might give me a few seconds' head start. Grabbing the lamp, I ran to the window, forced it open and prepared to drop onto the fire escape that I realised at the last minute wasn't there. Well, I did say it was a seedy hotel and safety regulations obviously weren't high on management's list of priorities. As I quickly tried to formulate a Plan B, there was a splintering noise from the opposite side of the room and the door was reduced to matchwood under the onslaught of a variety of crude swords and axes although, in fairness, you could probably have broken it down with a rubber knife without too much effort.

The horde swarmed into the room – or at least would have if they hadn't, yet again, fallen over each other in their eagerness to get me. It appeared that Madame Edna had placed a very high bounty on my head.

'There he is,' growled one, stating the very obvious as they could hardly have missed me sitting on the window ledge. 'Get him.'

There was only one thing for it. Taking a deep breath, I swung my legs over the ledge and threw myself at the neon sign. My luck was in and I managed to grab the crossbar of the letter 'T' in Humpty. My luck wasn't in for long, however, as, with a screech of metal, the whole letter detached from the wall and slowly fell outwards and downwards. Like a demented stuntman, with my skin glowing purple, I clung on for dear life wondering if the rest of the letters would stay fixed to the wall. My question was quickly answered as, to my total lack of surprise, the other letters advertising the hotel slowly peeled away from the hotel wall and down towards the ground in a gigantic neon arc.

On the street below, three Orcs that had obviously been asked to guard the hotel entrance looked up vacantly as I fell towards them. Taken completely by surprise, they didn't have time to get out of the way as a large glowing 'TY INN' and a purple-hued pig landed on them. For once I got lucky as I dropped on the largest and fattest of the Orcs and was exceedingly grateful for the soft landing. Unfortunately I didn't have the time to express my gratitude properly, seeing as the rest of his buddies were about to come charging out of the hotel in hot pursuit of my blood. In any event the poor guy was unconscious and I didn't have the luxury of enough time to even write a thank-you note; not that I would have anyway – I wasn't that grateful!

Checking to ensure I still had the lamp, I slowly got to my feet and raced – well, staggered actually – down the street. Seconds later, what was left of the Orc posse charged from the hotel and, spotting me limping towards the next intersection, howled in triumph as they ran after me.

I now had two objectives: evade my pursuers any way I possibly could and, assuming I was successful and didn't end up skewered by a large and rusty spear, get to an Internet café so I could send the most important email of my life.

I made the intersection and ran up the next street looking for something – anything – that might get the Orcs off my back. All I could see was the usual collection of seedy bars, dodgy clubs and occasional pawnshop that seemed to proliferate in the more disreputable parts of town. Despite my vain hope, there didn't appear to be any obvious cavalry-coming-over-the-hill-type rescue operation waiting for me. I had to admit it was looking grim. I could hear the grunts and shouts of the Orcs as they gained on me. Surely it was only a matter of seconds before I became a pork kebab.

Then I spotted it: a possible way out of my current predicament. Limping across the street, I staggered through the doors of the Tingling Finger Bar and Grill, hoping that the name reflected the nature of its clientele. I almost fell to my knees in relief (and pain and exhaustion) as every elf in the bar stopped what he was doing and stared at me in surprise.

Hanging on to the door for support with one arm, I indicated back over my shoulder with the other.

'Orcs,' I gasped. 'Following... me, trying... to... kill...'

I couldn't get any more out and clutched the door, trying to catch my breath.

Despite my semi-coherent gasping, they got the thrust of my message quickly enough. Then again, all they really needed to hear was 'Orc', as it tended to provoke an almost Pavlovian response when uttered in the presence of an elf. All the rest of the message was just supplemental information.

As any reader of fantasy fiction will tell you, Orcs and elves are sworn enemies. All it takes is for one to unexpectedly bump into the other at, say, a movie premiere for a small-scale war to break out. As a rule, hostilities usually only cease when one of the two opposing sides has been rendered totally unconscious – or worse.

It was no surprise, therefore, when my arrival resulted in the entire bar suddenly changing from a bunch of happy-go-lucky elves (if elves could ever be described as happy-go-lucky) trying unsuccessfully to get drunk to an efficient and very hostile fighting machine waiting for their enemy to burst through the door.

They didn't have long to wait, as the leading Orc pushed his way in, to be met by the heavily moisturised fist of the lead elf, the impact of which drove him back out again and into the arms of his colleagues.

'Orcs in the pub; blood will be spilled this night,' shouted one of the elves as he followed his leader outside to give both moral and physical support. Within seconds the bar was empty, apart from the barman and me. Like barmen the world over, he nodded at me and continued to clean glasses with a pristine white cloth as if nothing untoward had actually happened. Maybe his customers poured out of the bar every night in search of a row but I doubted it; elves usually preferred a quiet drink as opposed to a full-blooded brawl – except, that is, where Orcs were involved.

Still hurting, I staggered to the bar and looked up at the barman.

'Back... door?' I asked him.

He indicated a door at the back of the room with a brief twist of his head.

'Nearest... Internet... café?' Barmen usually knew everything about the locality; I just hoped this chap was one of them.

'Out the door; turn right; two blocks down. It's called the Cyber Punk. You can't miss it.'

I thanked him and struggled onwards out of the bar and down the street. The Cyber Punk was exactly where he described it. Looking around to confirm I was no longer being followed, I pushed the door open and made my way to the counter. A geeky goblin (the actual Cyber Punk presumably) sat behind it, glancing through a magazine. I waved a twenty under his nose to get his attention. He looked down at me over glasses that were so thick they could have been used as bullet-proof windows.

'I need to access the web,' I said to him and waved the twenty from side to side. His head moved back and forth tracking every movement, his eyes never leaving the money.

'Pick any one you want,' he said slowly reaching for the bill.

Picking a terminal at the back of the room, where I was less likely to be seen from the street, I accessed one of my many email accounts. I began to carefully compose the most important email I was probably ever going to send. After typing furiously for a few minutes, I reviewed what I had written. I hoped it was enough to get the attention of the recipient without giving too much away to anyone else that might intercept it.

Dear Criminal Mastermind,

I know who you are and why you stole the lamp. I understand your need for complete secrecy, although transporting me to your hideout ultimately gave the game away (and employing Benny certainly didn't help your cause, either). To prove I know what's going on, I offer you this: he who controls the third option controls the power. It may be cryptic but I think you'll understand what I mean.

I think I can help you. Be prepared to be present at the original drop point early tomorrow morning and take your cue from me. If all goes to plan we may both find ourselves out of this sorry mess for once and for all.

Best regards,

Harry Pigg

After a moment's panic when I couldn't remember it, I typed in the address Benny had used previously (evilgenius@ criminalmasterminds.com), hit the send button and my email disappeared from the screen. All I needed to do now was to get the other two players in this dangerous game to meet me tomorrow, and hope I could pull off a very elaborate stunt.

If I was successful, then I would be free of any unpleasant entanglements forever. If not, then I was likely to be caught in a very unsavoury Aladdin and Edna sandwich – with me as the filling.

I borrowed a phone from the Cyber Punk and, with a certain degree of trepidation, I made two very nervous calls. With nowhere else to go, I spent the rest of the night in the Cyber Punk, alternately surfing the web and playing World of Warcraft.

12

A Gripping Finale

E ven early in the morning, Wilde Park was busy.
The Three Blind Mice were begging as usual at the
main gate. Fairy godmothers fussed around their
charges, making sure they were well wrapped up against the
morning chill as they played on the swings. An occasional
elf jogger in pastel Lycra running gear panted along the
pathways. Show-offs – always more concerned with looking
good than actually keeping fit.

I had picked the most public area I could find for my
dangerous rendezvous: a large open area with a small
clump of trees to one side. Hidden in the trees was a very
nervous Jack.

I had called him first thing and briefed him on the plan.
He wasn't going to be in any danger but his role was critical.
Precise timing was essential so I drilled him over and over
on his instructions.

'You sure you know what to do?' I asked him as we
walked towards the bushes.

'For goodness sake, Mr Pigg, we've gone over it twenty

129

times. Just give me the lamp.' Grabbing it from my hands he forced his way into the bushes and crouched down.

'Just wait for my signal, OK?' I said to him as I walked away. 'And keep yourself hidden until then.'

He gave me a thumbs-up sign and disappeared from view. I walked to the middle of the park and looked back. Satisfied that he couldn't be detected, I stood where anyone entering could see me and waited.

I didn't have to wait long. There was a loud rumbling from above and a helicopter flew low over the trees. It circled the park twice and then landed close to me, the blast of wind from the rotors covering me in dust, potato chip packets and candy wrappers. This case had certainly found diverse and interesting ways of getting me dirty.

Peeling away a potato chip packet that had stuck to my forehead, I watched as Aladdin and my good friend Gruff alighted from the 'copter. The wind from the rotors didn't appear to affect Aladdin in the slightest. Nothing stuck to his suit, and his hair moved so little it must have been glued to his head. If nothing else, the man had style in spades.

'Mr Aladdin.' I stretched out my trotter. 'Glad you could make it at such short notice.' I didn't acknowledge Gruff and, strangely, he didn't offer to shake my trotter either.

Aladdin gave my trotter a perfunctory shake. 'Mr Pigg. I assume from your call that you have my lamp.'

'It's nearby and very safe,' I replied. 'Please be patient and you'll have it back shortly.'

From the look he gave me, patience clearly wasn't going to be top of Aladdin's order of business for the day. I hoped that Edna was going to arrive soon as I didn't know how long Aladdin's fuse was.

Fortunately, the Wicked Witch of the West Side was as anxious to recover the lamp as everyone else. A long line of stretch limos snaked from the main entrance of the park to where we waited. A small army (in both size and number) of henchOrcs disgorged from the cars and took up positions around us.

Two very large minders in black tuxedos and sunglasses squeezed themselves out of a large black Merc and stood beside the rear door as Edna made her entrance. These bodyguards exuded menace and were the kind of muscle that would still look intimidating dressed in pink tutus. They stood at either side of Edna as she walked towards us, their faces (at least what I could see of them behind the shades) expressionless. When they got closer I could see they were actually gorillas (as in silverbacks and mutual grooming). Clearly Edna relied on minders that were a little bit more effective than Ogre Security (Not On Our Watch). Her gorillas were the genuine article.

Aladdin and Edna both eyed each other warily. Clearly both wanted to know what the other was doing here, but neither was going to be the first to ask. They had their pride. I let them posture and sweat for a bit longer just to show who was nominally in charge, but primarily because I was thinking of a thousand ways how my plan (which seemed so foolproof last night) might, in the light of day, actually blow up in my face now that all the key players were here.

Edna broke the silence first.

'Harry Pigg again,' she sneered. 'And smelling so much nicer than when we last met. Care to tell me what we're all doing here?'

'A very good question, Mr Pigg.' Aladdin looked at me steadily. 'More to the point, do you have my lamp?'

'*Your* lamp?' exclaimed Edna, turning her attention to Aladdin. 'No way, pal. It's my lamp.'

Aladdin took a step towards her and the two bouncers suddenly appeared in front of him, blocking his way. I was interested to see that Gruff was keeping himself a safe distance away from his master, which was quite understandable, considering the size of Edna's minders, but hardly a career-enhancing move. Unless he backed up his employer, it was quite possible his next job could be propping up a bridge – from inside the concrete support. Mr Aladdin had certain expectations of his employees.

'Ma'am,' said Aladdin, raising his hands in a conciliatory gesture, 'I assure you the lamp is mine. In fact, I employed Mr Pigg here,' and he waved an arm in my direction, 'to locate it for me.' He looked at me again. 'And you have found it, haven't you?' he said levelly. 'Because I really hope you didn't bring me to this accursed place at this unearthly hour of the day for any other reason.'

Despite my best effort I was now the centre of attention and that was the last place I wanted to be. Beads of sweat formed on my brow.

Edna took a few steps towards me. 'Well, Pigg, is this true? Is it his lamp?'

I coughed nervously and cleared my throat.

'OK folks,' I stammered. 'Let me explain. Now if you could all step back a small bit and give me some room, I'll begin.'

I didn't really need the room; I just wanted to be able to see where Jack was hiding.

Everyone shuffled back slowly, muttering and giving me foul looks. If this didn't work, chances were I'd become the booby prize in a turf-war between Aladdin and Edna and I really didn't fancy my head being mounted over the fireplace of the winner.

'Ladies, gentlemen, foul-smelling Orcs, very muscular simian bodyguards and offensive goat,' I began. 'Let me tell you a little story.

'Once upon a time, a very rich man had a magic lamp that he treasured above all else. One night the lamp was stolen by person or persons unknown and, through a series of bizarre circumstances, ended up in the hands of another of our foremost citizens.' I nodded towards Edna, who just continued to scowl at me.

I know, I know; I was piling it on with a trowel but I had to keep both of them sweet for a little while longer.

'Now this lady,' I nodded at Edna, the word 'lady' sticking in my throat, 'assumed that the lamp was now her property, possession being nine-tenths of the law and all that.

'Unfortunately, the original owner of the lamp employed the town's foremost detective to track it down and return it.' For some reason there was much coughing, clearing of throats and disbelieving glances at this statement – I can't imagine why.

'Through prodigious feats of deduction,' more coughing, 'he tracked down and recovered the missing lamp and can now return it to its rightful owner.'

I looked straight at where Jack was hiding and nodded my head. I caught a glimpse of him as he bent down and began to cover the lamp in mud. When the lamp was liberally smeared, he cautiously made his way towards me, holding it carefully in both hands.

'Tell me, Mr Aladdin,' I asked, 'what do you most wish for right now?'

As I waited for his reply, I took the lamp from Jack and handed it to him. He looked at it aghast.

'For goodness sake, Pigg. Could you not have cleaned it before you handed it back?'

Reaching into his pocket, he grabbed a handkerchief and began cleaning the lamp.

I was sweating profusely now – like a pig, in fact. The success of my plan depended on the next few minutes.

'I'm sorry, Mr Aladdin, I just hadn't time. I wanted to get

it back to you as soon as I could. But you haven't answered my question.'

He continued rubbing the lamp furiously, oblivious to the plume of white smoke that was beginning to pour from the nozzle.

'Oh yes, your question,' he said. 'What I really wish for most right now is to find out who stole my lamp and why.'

There was a loud crack and the white smoke solidified into a very large and very happy-looking genie – all turban, silk trousers and a cone of smoke where his feet should have been.

'BEHOLD, I AM THE GENIE OF THE LAMP,' he bellowed. 'AND YOUR THIRD WISH SHALL BE GRANTED. IT WAS I WHO STOLE YOUR LAMP.'

Aladdin looked at him in horror and with dawning comprehension. He'd been had.

I turned quickly to Jack while everyone was looking in astonishment at the genie.

'Jack, now!' I roared.

Quickly, Jack ran to Aladdin and, before he could react, had grabbed the lamp and flung it at me. Catching it skilfully, I quickly rubbed it again.

The genie looked at me and his smile grew even broader.

'I AM THE GENIE OF THE LAMP. YOU HAVE THREE WISHES. WHAT IS YOUR BIDDING, MY MASTER?'

I took a deep breath and in a very loud voice – to ensure everyone could hear – outlined my first wish.

'I wish that if, as a result of this case, any harm should come to me or any of my associates at the hands of either Aladdin or Edna, or anyone connected with them for that matter, both will suffer cruel and unusual punishment – such punishment at the genie's discretion.' Granted, it was a mouthful but I needed to cover all the bases.

The genie bowed deeply.

'YOUR WISH IS GRANTED.'

From the horrified look on their faces, I could see that both Edna and Aladdin clearly understood what had happened. I was safe from any retaliation by either of them and, in the context of what had happened in this case, that had understandably been my first priority. I was untouchable – at least by them – and was savouring the moment. But I wasn't finished yet.

'My second wish is that, after thousands of years of imprisonment at the hands of selfish masters, the genie is to set himself free.'

The genie bowed even more deeply and waved his arms theatrically – obviously playing to his audience.

'YOUR WISH IS GRANTED.'

As he said this, the smoke began to drift away on the wind and, from his knees down, the rest of his legs began to materialise. Slowly he descended to the ground and landed carefully, testing his balance. Satisfied that he could at least stand without falling over (if not actually walk) he smiled at me and nodded his gratitude.

'I thank you, sir, from the bottom of my heart. For too long have I been in thrall to masters who have used me for their own devices with no thought for my wishes. Now I am free and shall be no man's slave from here on in.'

I didn't want to point out to him that now that he was free he'd have to get a job. I wondered what skills he did have but imagined that being an ex-genie wouldn't necessarily endear him to potential employers. I also noticed that he wasn't shouting in block capitals any more – presumably another advantage of being a free man, and one that wasn't quite as hard on the ears of anyone within a ten-mile radius.

As he spoke I noticed Edna nod to her gorillas. They surreptitiously made their way towards me, trying (not very successfully it has to be said) to be unobtrusive. As they advanced I began to back away ever so slowly. As I did so, the genie shook his head and, with a slight wave of his hand, motioned for me to stop.

I gave him a 'you must be joking; have you seen who's coming after me' look but he nodded more emphatically. As he did so I noticed that as the heavies got to about ten feet from me, they suddenly shrank to the size of garden gnomes. I suddenly became very brave and raised my foot to stomp down on them. Squealing in fear they ran back towards Edna and, as they did so, they quickly grew back to their original height. My enthusiasm for squashing them evaporated, primarily because they were now more than capable of squashing me first.

I looked at the genie in confusion.

'It's very simple,' he said. 'Even though I'm free and no longer capable of magic, any spell I've already cast remains in force. If either of them,' he nodded at Edna and Aladdin, 'tries to harm you, or employs someone to do so, they will suffer most unpleasant consequences indeed.'

I smiled at my sudden invulnerability.

'Of course,' he continued, 'that won't stop you from being harmed by anyone else.'

The smile disappeared as fast as it had arrived. Typical, I thought – there's always a downside. Mind you, at least I was safe from the two people currently most likely to do me harm – both of whom, along with their respective entourages, were backing away quietly from me so as not to incur any further pain or humiliation.

I couldn't resist it; I ran quickly towards them. It was one of the finest moments of my life. Imagine, if you will, one very fat oriental gentleman, a goat, two large gorillas in tuxedos, a disorganised swarm of Orcs, and Edna (who had trouble walking let alone moving any faster) all desperately clambering backwards over each other in a frantic effort to get as far away from me as they could. The resulting scrum made me laugh out loud for the first time in quite a while.

I think it was at that point I realised that the case was more or less over. All I needed to do was tie up a few loose ends and explain to Jack what had happened.

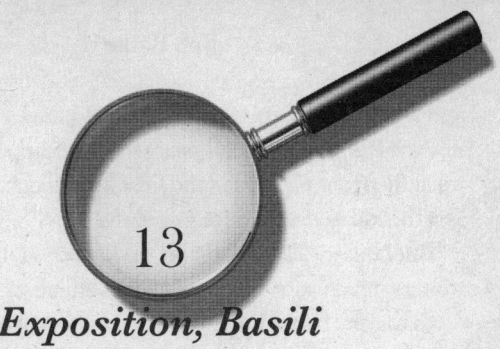

13

Exposition, Basili

'**B**ut how did you know it was the genie?' Jack asked.

The three of us – Jack, the genie and I – were in my office, sitting around my desk drinking coffee. Much as I'd like to take all the credit for solving the case – being a famous detective and all – if Jack hadn't turned up at Edna's wielding the leg from a suit of armour, chances are I'd have ended up a permanent face-down resident in the sewers I'd come to love so much. The least he deserved was an explanation.

The genie, on the other hand, was just hanging around. Now that he was homeless, seeing as he couldn't fit into his lamp any more, he had latched on to me – and it was placing me in a very difficult position.

In my job, I needed to be discreet, and discretion was going to be very difficult when you were being shadowed by a large dark-skinned ex-genie whose idea of sartorial elegance was a bright yellow turban, a yellow and red patterned waistcoat that seemed twenty sizes too small and a pair of baggy yellow silk trousers that ended just above the ankles and looked like someone had inflated a large hot-air balloon in each leg. On his feet a pair of yellow slippers that curled up at the front just added the final lurid touch.

Oh, and he farted a lot – an awful lot.

But I digress. Elbows on my desk, I rested my head on my trotters, made sure I had everyone's attention and began.

'It was the lamp. I'd stared at it for most of the night trying to figure out why it seemed so familiar. Then, just as I was on the point of giving up, I went to bed and it struck me.'

'The bed struck you?' said Jack. 'How?'

'No, not the bed,' I replied wearily. 'An idea. I suddenly realised where I'd seen it before and why it had taken so long to work it out. I'd seen it from the inside.'

'Huh?' The look on Jack's face said it all.

'It was when I was in that white room. The curved walls were the same shape as the body of the lamp. I'd been pulled into it by our friend Basili here,' I said, nodding at the genie. 'Of course, I didn't know it at the time; I just thought I'd been taken prisoner by an insane interior decorator.

'Once I figured that the genie was looking for his own lamp, it all began to fall into place.'

I could see the confusion on Jack's face and held up a warning trotter before he could ask another 'why' or 'how' question.

'When I rubbed the lamp, nothing happened,' I continued. 'My first reaction was that it was all a hoax and the lamp was exactly that: a lamp; with no magic, no three wishes and no genie. No offence.' I looked across the table at the genie.

'None taken,' he replied calmly.

'Then I figured that if the last owner hadn't used up all his wishes yet, then rubbing the lamp would probably have no effect. However, once the three wishes had been granted then the lamp was up for grabs again, making it a very valuable antique indeed.'

The genie nodded his agreement.

'This would explain why Aladdin had kept the lamp so securely under lock and key. As long as he had it, he still had a last wish, but it was useless to anyone else unless they could get him to use up that last wish.

'Now, if you were the genie that provided this somewhat unique service, I imagine that it would get quite tedious, if not downright frustrating, being stuck in a lamp with no way of getting out, just sitting there waiting for that last rub to happen.'

I turned to Basili. 'How long were you waiting after Aladdin's second wish?'

The genie heaved a deep sigh. 'Forty years.'

'Wow!' exclaimed Jack. 'You were stuck in there for forty years? What did you do to pass the time?'

'Initially, I read, watched TV and ate a lot,' said Basili. From his size, it didn't need a detective to work that out. 'Then with the arrival of the computer age and the information superhighway, I learned everything about PCs and used them to interface with the outside world, looking for an opportunity to set myself free.'

'Which is how he met Benny,' I said.

'Poor Benny,' said Basili with a sympathetic shake of the head and a loud fart. 'I'm sorry about that but he was my only option.'

'Don't worry, he's probably already forgotten about it. Gnomes have a very short attention span.' I looked at the genie. 'What I want to know is how you managed to find out so much about security systems?'

Basili's grin was so wide his head looked like it was split in two. In fact, I don't believe he'd actually stopped smiling since he'd been freed. 'Hacking.'

'Hacking?' I repeated stupidly.

'Yes, hacking. With twenty years of computer experience, I was at the cutting edge of cyber crime from the word go. There isn't a system out there I can't crack. Aladdin's just needed a bit of time. Once I had access, it was easy to figure out where the weaknesses were. I just wish I'd picked someone brighter to actually steal the lamp.' There was another loud rumble from his side of the desk, which I hoped was his stomach telling him it was hungry. A few moments later that hope was cruelly dashed and I walked over to the window to let some fresher air in. Basili gave me another apologetic look.

I figured it was about time I took back control of the conversation and make myself the centre of attention once more. I walked back to the desk and looked at the other two.

'Once I figured that the genie was the one who was calling the shots, or at least one of the three calling the shots, I thought that if I could strike a deal with him I might get the other two off my back – assuming he was willing to play ball.'

'And I was,' grinned Basili. Paarp! Phut-phut-phut-phut! 'All I wanted was someone to help me gain my freedom and Mr Harry here was most anxious to help me, as well as himself.'

I nodded furiously. 'Using the same email address Benny had used, I told him that I knew who he was and proved it by cryptically suggesting that the person who controlled the third wish effectively controlled the genie. If the message was understood then all he had to do was follow my lead at Wilde Park when I was hopefully going to make him appear.' I smiled at the memory of the look on Aladdin's face when he realised he'd been duped. 'Fortunately for us all, everything went more or less according to plan. Basili was set free and I got Aladdin and Edna off my back. Unfortunately, as I was no longer flavour of the month with Aladdin, he declined to pay me for my services.'

As usual things hadn't panned out yet again for the proprietor of the Third Pig Detective Agency. Then again, I was getting used to it. This time, however, I had also picked up a stray – a very large, yellow stray that, partly thanks to me, no longer had a home.

To my surprise (and embarrassment) Basili stood up, walked around the desk to me and gave me a big hug. It was the kind of hug that large bears used to crush their prey but he managed to break off before any major organs were ruptured. Struggling for breath, I dropped back into my chair.

'It is not so big a problem, Mr Harry.' His smile was even broader. I suspected that both ends met at the back of his head. 'While I waited in my lamp for all those years, I also used my computer to play the market. I have been very successful and have built up a most valuable and highly diverse portfolio. Perhaps I can recompense you somewhat for your efforts in this matter.'

If this had been a cartoon, my jaw would have bounced off the ground in surprise. I struggled to get words out. 'You mean, you're rich?' I gasped.

'But of course,' Basili replied. 'How else would I have been able to help Benny with his most audacious plans for the theme park? I insist that you be paid for the most successful resolution of this case.' He thought for a moment. 'Hey, maybe I can become your backer – like Charlie in Charlie's Angels.'

I was about to point out that I looked nothing like any of Charlie's Angels when I became aware of a commotion from reception. Two voices were raised in argument. One was clearly Gloria's but the other was unfamiliar and very loud, very female and very commanding. For one awful minute I thought Edna or one of her sisters had come to 'pay me a visit', but the voice sounded a little more cultured than those of the Wicked Witch sisters so I relaxed a little – but not too much.

'But you don't have an appointment,' I could hear Gloria say.

'Nevertheless, I must see him,' said the other voice, in a tone that suggested she wasn't used to being obstructed. She didn't realise that she was being obstructed by the best. If she managed to get past Gloria, she deserved an appointment.

'No appointment, no meeting,' said Gloria emphatically. 'Mr Pigg is a very busy detective and can't afford to have his time wasted. If you care to make an appointment, I can organise a suitable time.'

'No way, lady,' came the reply. 'I know he's in that office and I am going in to see him now. Please do not get in my way.'

Now I was starting to get scared. What kind of monster was in my reception area and why did she want to see me? More to the point, did I really want to see her?

I could see that Jack and Basili were giving me anxious looks as well. We all started to back away from the door slowly and quietly. In hindsight there wasn't really any point. The only thing behind us was the window; we were on the third floor and there was no fire escape.

Note to self: speak to new landlord about fire safety regulations.

Through the frosted glass I could see a large red shape move towards the door.

'Do not go in there,' shouted Gloria.

'Try and stop me, lady.' There was a sound of scuffling and then the door burst open, banging off the wall with a loud crash.

A very large lady dressed in black boots, bright red trousers and a hooded red jacket stood there. Gloria was clinging on to one of her legs. She had clearly been dragged across the room in her efforts to keep this person out.

'Sorry, Harry,' she gasped. 'She got by me when I wasn't looking.'

'It's OK, Gloria,' I said and walked over to her to help her up. 'Let's see what this lady wants that's so urgent.'

I looked at the new arrival. Her face was as red as the clothing she was wearing – presumably from her altercation with Gloria. White fur lined the cuffs of her jacket and rimmed her hood. For some reason her appearance suggested Christmas.

I indicated one of the seats recently vacated by my colleagues.

'Ma'am,' I said, turning on the charm, 'if you'd care to sit down.'

As she sat I turned to the others. 'If I could perhaps speak to this fine lady alone,' I suggested. Gloria nodded and, grabbing the other two by the arm, dragged them both out of the office before they could protest.

I nodded towards the door as they left. 'My partners. They may not look like much but they've got it where it counts.'

As I spoke, I realised that they had indeed become partners, either by virtue of the help one had given or the financial backing the other was offering. Looked like the Third Pig Detective Agency was expanding.

I turned to my newest prospective client.

'Now then,' I said. 'How may the Third Pig Detective Agency be of help, Miss, Mrs, Ms...?'

'Claus. It's Mrs Claus and I need you to find my husband. He's been kidnapped and it's only two days to 25th December. If he's not found soon we may have to cancel Christmas.'

The End

The Third Pig Detective Agency will return
in
The Ho Ho Ho Mystery

Acknowledgements

This book's formative years were spent on the web so huge thanks go to all at Writelink for the initial encouragement and those at YouWriteOn – especially Edward Smith and Michael Legat – whose critiques (good, bad and otherwise – but always constructive) helped shape the opening chapters into something approaching legibility.

I owe a lot to the good people at the Friday Project: especially Scott, whose unflagging belief in Harry's adventures and championing of the cause kept the book alive when things didn't look so good.

Thanks to Dooradoyle and Adare Libraries for providing a quiet corner to write in and to Carol Anderson for a wonderful copy-edit.

I also owe a debt of gratitude to my parents who instilled a love of reading in me at a very young age. This is all your fault!

Above all, huge thanks go to my wife Gemma and my three boys, Ian, Adam and Stephen, whose support, belief, encouragement and the occasional 'get back in there and write another chapter now' made all this worthwhile.

151

No, Ian, we won't be getting a Gulfstream jet with the proceeds. Yes, Adam, the book will be in the shops. No, Stephen, you can't have your tea – you only had your dinner an hour ago.

Harry would like to thank the Big Bad Wolf, for giving him that first big break; Little Red Riding Hood, for not appearing in this book and making a show of herself; Jack Horner, for the pizza (you know what I'm talking about!) and his legions of fans – he knows you're out there somewhere, you just haven't made yourself known to him yet.